# FRENCH
# EXIT

# FRENCH EXIT

## A TRAGEDY OF MANNERS

# PATRICK DeWITT

ANANSI

Published in Canada in 2018 by House of Anansi Press Inc.
www.houseofanansi.com

House of Anansi Press is committed to protecting our natural environment. As part of our efforts, the interior of this book is printed on paper that contains 100% post-consumer recycled fibres, is acid-free, and is processed chlorine-free.

22 21 20 19 18   1 2 3 4 5

Library and Archives Canada Cataloguing in Publication

DeWitt, Patrick, 1975–, author
French exit / Patrick deWitt.

Issued in print and electronic formats.
ISBN 978-1-4870-0483-5 (softcover).—ISBN 978-1-4870-0484-2
(EPUB).—ISBN 978-1-4870-0485-9 (Kindle)

I. Title.

PS8607.E9825F74 2018       C813'.6       C2018-900703-6
                            C2018-900704-4

Book design: Suet Yee Chong
Cover illustrations: Eric Hanson

We acknowledge for their financial support of our publishing program
the Canada Council for the Arts, the Ontario Arts Council, and the Government of Canada.

Printed and bound in Canada

RECYCLED
Paper made from
recycled material
FSC® C103567

*For Rachel*

Ah, the unconquerable past!

—OSCAR LEVANT

# NEW YORK

# 1.

"All good things must end," said Frances Price.

She was a moneyed, striking woman of sixty-five years, easing her hands into black calfskin gloves on the steps of a brownstone in New York City's Upper East Side. Her son, Malcolm, thirty-two, stood nearby looking his usual broody and unkempt self. It was late autumn, dusk; the windows of the brownstone were lit, a piano sounded on the air—a tasteful party was occurring. Frances was explaining her early departure to a similarly wealthy though less lovely individual, this the hostess. Her name doesn't matter. She was aggrieved.

"You're certain you have to go? Is it really so bad as that?"

"According to the veterinarian it's only a matter of time," Frances said. "What a shame. We were having such a lovely evening."

"Were you really?" the hostess asked hopefully.

"Such a lovely evening. And I do hate to leave. But it sounds an actual emergency, and what can be done in the face of that?"

The hostess considered her answer. "Nothing," she said finally. A silence arrived; to Frances's horror, the hostess lunged and clung to her. "I've always admired you so," she whispered.

"Malcolm," said Frances.

"Actually I'm sort of afraid of you. Is that very silly of me?"

"Malcolm, Malcolm."

Malcolm found the hostess pliable; he peeled her away from his mother, then took the woman's hand in his and shook it. She watched her hand going up and down with an expression of puzzlement. She'd had two too many drinks and there was nothing in her stomach but a viscous pâté. She returned to her home and Malcolm led Frances away, down the steps to the sidewalk. They passed the waiting town car and sat on a bench twenty yards back from the brownstone, for there was no emergency, no veterinarian, and the cat, that antique oddity called Small Frank, was not unwell, so far as they knew.

Frances lit a cigarette with her gold lighter. She liked this lighter best due to its satisfying weight, and the distinguished *click!* it made at the moment of ignition. She aimed the glowing cherry at the hostess, now visible in an upstairs window, speaking with one of her guests. Frances shook her head. "Born to bore."

Malcolm was inspecting a framed photograph he'd stolen from the hostess's bedroom. "She's just drunk. Hopefully she won't remember in the morning."

"She'll send flowers if she does." Frances took up the photograph, a recent studio portrait of the hostess. Her head was tilted back, her mouth ajar, a frantic happiness in her eyes. Frances ran her finger along the edge of the ornate frame. "Is this jade?"

"I think it is," said Malcolm.

"It's very beautiful," she said, and handed it back to Malcolm. He opened the frame and removed the photo, folding it in crisp quarters and dropping it into a trash can beside their bench. He returned the frame to his coat pocket and resumed his study of the party, pointing out a late-middle-aged man with a cummerbund encasing a markedly round stomach. "That man's some type of ambassador."

"Yes, and if those epaulets could talk."

"Did you speak to his wife?"

Frances nodded. "Men's teeth in a child's mouth. I had to look away." She flicked her cigarette into the street.

"Now what," Malcolm said.

A vagrant approached and stood before them. His eyes were bright with alcohol and he asked in a chirpy voice, "Got anything to spare tonight, folks?" Malcolm was leaning in to shoo the man when Frances caught his arm. "It's possible that we do," she said. "But may we ask what you need the money *for*?"

"Oh, you know." The man raised and dropped his arms. "Just getting by."

"Could you please be more specific?"

"I guess I'd like a little wine, if you want to know."

He swayed in place, and Frances asked him, in a confiding voice, "Is it possible you've already had something to drink tonight?"

"I got my edges smoothed," the man admitted.

"And what does that mean?"

"Means I had a drink before, but now I'm thinking about another."

Frances appreciated the answer. "What's your name?"

"Dan."

"May I call you Daniel?"

"If that's what you want to do."

"What's your preferred brand of wine, Daniel?"

"I'll drink anything wet, ma'am. But I do like that Three Roses."

"And how much for a bottle of Three Roses?"

"A bottle's five bucks. A gallon's eight." He shrugged as if to say the gallon was the shrewd consumer's choice.

"And what would you buy if I gave you twenty dollars?"

"Twenty dollars," said Dan, and he whistled a puff of dry air. "For twenty dollars I could get two gallons of Three Roses and a weenie." He patted the pocket of his army coat. "I already got my cigarettes."

"The twenty would set you up nicely, then?"

"Oh, quite nicely."

"And where would you bring it all? Back to your room?"

Dan squinted. He was realizing the scenario in his mind. "The weenie I'd eat on the spot. The wine and the cigarettes, I'd take those into the park with me. That's where I sleep most nights, in the park."

"Where in the park?"

"Under a bush."

"A particular bush?"

"A bush is a bush, in my experiment. Experience."

Frances smiled sweetly at Dan. "All right," she said. "So, you'd lie under a bush in the park, and you'd smoke your cigarettes and drink your red wine."

"Yeah."

"You'd look up at the stars."

"Why not."

Frances said, "Would you really drink both gallons in a night?"

"Yeah, yes, I surely would."

"Wouldn't you feel awful in the morning?"

"That's what mornings are for, ma'am."

He'd spoken without comedic intent, and Frances thought that Dan's mornings were probably wretched beyond her comprehension. Sufficiently touched, she opened her clutch and fished out twenty dollars. Dan received the bill, shuddered from skull to toe, then walked off at an apparently painfully brisk pace. A beat cop approached, looking after Dan with malice.

"That guy wasn't bothering you two I hope?"

"Who, Daniel?" said Frances. "Not at all. He's a friend of ours."

"Seemed like he was putting the bite on you."

Frances stared icily. "Actually, I was paying him back. I should have paid him back a long time ago, but Dan's been very patient with me. I thank God for the fact of a man like him. Not that it's any of *your* business." She held up the lighter and lit it: *click!* The flame, stubby and blue-bottomed, was positioned between them, as though defining a border. A sense of isolation came over the cop and he wandered away, asking sorry, small questions to himself. Frances turned to Malcolm and clapped her hands together, communicating a job is done sentiment. They disliked policemen; indeed, they disliked all figures of authority.

"Have you had enough?" asked Malcolm.

"I've," answered Frances.

Walking toward the town car, she took up Malcolm's arm in her special-loving-creature manner. "Home," she told the driver.

The grand, multilevel apartment was dim, and resembled a museum after hours. The cook had left them a roast in the oven; Malcolm plated two portions and they ate in silence, which was not the norm, but they were both distracted by personal unhappinesses. Malcolm was worrying about Susan, his fiancée. He hadn't seen her in several days and the last time they'd spoken she had called him a rude and vulgar name. Frances's concern was existential; she lately had found herself mired in an eerie feeling, as one standing with her back to the ocean. Small Frank, elderly to the point of decrepitude, clambered onto the table and sat before Frances. She and the cat stared at each other. Frances lit a cigarette and exhaled a column of smoke into his face. He winced and left the room.

Malcolm said, "What's tomorrow?"

"Mr. Baker insists on a meeting," Frances answered. Mr. Baker was their financial adviser, and had been the executor of the estate after the death of Frances's husband, Malcolm's father, Franklin Price.

"What's he want?" asked Malcolm.

"He wouldn't say."

This was not, technically, a lie—Mr. Baker hadn't stated explicitly what the meeting was about. But Frances knew all too well what he wished to discuss with her. The thought of it made her morose, and she excused herself, ascending the marble staircase to curry solace in a bath choked with miniature pearlescent bubbles. Afterward she sat on the settee in the bathroom, in her plush robe, and her hair was down, Small Frank sleeping at her feet. She was speaking with Joan on the phone.

# 2.

They had met five decades earlier, at an all-girls' summer camp in Connecticut. Joan was new money and everyone was aghast at her lack of refinement, her apparent disinterest in self-improvement. Frances was the most popular girl there, handily; vast energies were expended daily that her friendship might be won. She was bored by this, and became fixated on Joan, admiring her gracelessness, her scuffed kneecaps, her scowl. In the cafeteria one afternoon all looked on as Frances moved to sit with Joan, a piece of chocolate cake in each hand. Joan eyed the dessert with suspicion.

"What's this?" she said.

"One for you, one for me."

"Why?"

"Just being decent, I guess. Why don't you unscrew your face and have a bite?" Frances took a bite herself; Joan followed after. Over the course of the consumption of the cake, Joan became emotional, and the moment she finished she hurried from the cafeteria, fearful she might cry from the fact of Frances's kindness, and she did cry, in the forest by the lake where a loon came in for a wake-making landing on the polished silver water. That night, at the campfire sing-a-song, Joan sat next to Frances, and Frances smiled at her and touched her knee to welcome her into her life.

Their friendship began with a pistol shot, it seemed; they loved each other from the start and it had been this way all the time since. Now, so many years later, Joan was the only one Frances could be herself with, though this isn't accurately stated since it wasn't as if Frances suddenly unleashed her hidden being once Joan arrived. Let it be said instead that she did, in Joan's company, become a person she was only with Joan—a person she liked becoming. Joan had many friends, but beyond Malcolm, Frances had only Joan.

She, Frances, was looking out the high window above her vanity and into the black cube of sky. A leaf wandered drunkenly past. "It used to be that seasons filled me with expectation," she said. "Now they seem more a hostile encroachment."

Joan was perusing a catalog in bed. "I thought we'd agreed not to talk about death at night." She flipped a page. "Christmas is coming. I say it each year, but you're hell to shop for."

"I'm simple: I want nothing." Frances had come to think of gift-giving as a polite form of witchcraft. Another leaf bobbed past her window and a chill took her. She was wrestling with the thought of whether or not to discuss her problem with Joan. She had decided she would when there occurred an unexplainable event, which was that a sleek black lizard, ten inches from nose to tail, shot from behind the toilet and breezed over the tops of her bare feet before continuing on into the bedroom. Frances hung up the phone, crossed the room, and closed the door to shut herself in. She returned to the phone, picked it up, and called Malcolm, who was in bed down the hall, staring at the telephone and wondering why Susan wasn't calling him, but also why he wasn't calling Susan. He jumped when it rang.

"Malcolm," Frances whispered.

"Oh, hello, there. Did you miss me, or what?"

"Listen to me. There's a lizard dashing around my bedroom and I need you to come down here and do something about it."

"A lizard? How'd that happen?"

"I don't understand the question. It walked in of its own accord. Will you come, yes or no?"

"You want me to?"

"I want you to. Also I want you to want to."

"Well, I guess I'd better come, then," said Malcolm.

Soon he entered Frances's bedroom. She spoke from behind the bathroom door: "Do you see it?"

"No."

"Stomp around a bit."

Malcolm stomped about the room but there was no sign of the lizard. Knowing his mother would accept nothing less than unassailable proof of the reptile's demise or departure, he constructed a plan to set her mind at ease. He opened a window and waited awhile. "You can come out, now," he said. "It's gone."

Frances's face appeared in the doorway. "Gone where?"

"Wherever lizards go—it's not for us to know."

She crept across the carpet and to his elbow. Malcolm explained about the window and she asked, "You saw him run out?"

"He took it at a sprint."

"You're very good," she told him, squeezing his arm.

"It wasn't much."

"You're very good and clever."

But now the lizard emerged from beneath Frances's bed, approaching them in halting zigzags. It stood at their feet performing important push-ups and Frances returned to the bathroom, closing the door behind her. "Please will you pack me a bag," she said, "and one for yourself, and I'll meet you downstairs in fifteen minutes."

He did as he was told and soon found her in the lobby, explaining to the doorman about the lizard. Her hair was up, her cheeks faintly rouged; she wore a long black-and-red-checked wool coat to cover her pajamas, and ballet slippers on her feet. She took up her suitcase and exited the building, Malcolm following behind her. They registered at the Four Seasons and retired to their respective suites.

Frances ordered two martinis from room service. When they arrived she set them on the bedside table, admiring their twin-ness for a time, then she drank them. Failing to take any water before sleep she had parched visions all through the night: a juicy plum eluded her, passed from hand to hand in some person-thick open-air-market dream environment. Upon waking she once again called room service, requesting that which she could not have in slumber. The plum was delivered on a heavy, filigreed tray. She sat in the center of her overlarge, sunlit bed and ate it, hopeful for a valid experience, but it erred on the dry side, possessed no magic, and did nothing to lessen much less solve her deeper difficulties. This was unfortunate but unsurprising and she didn't let the fruit's failure influence her mood. Bracing herself, she called Mr. Baker, who wasn't available to answer, mercifully. She left a false but believable message explaining that she was indisposed and so unable to meet that day. Returning home in the early afternoon, the doorman presented Malcolm and Frances with a couriered letter as well as an outsize floral bouquet. Frances sniffed the flowers and asked, "Who has died, and what was their purpose, and did they fulfill their potential?" The doorman didn't hazard a response. Frances made him uneasy; he believed there was something quite wrong with her.

"Any lizard news?" she asked.

"Yes, Mrs. Price. That's the end of that."

"You killed it?"

"Yeah."

"You personally?"

"Personally I killed it."

"What was the killing style?"

"Foot killing. I've got it in a box if you want to take a look."

"I'll pass, with thanks and sad regrets. Please will you carry the flowers, Malcolm?"

The letter was from Mr. Baker. Frances read it to herself while she and Malcolm waited for the elevator. *Frances, enough of this. It's past time and you know it's past time. I'll be at the Grotto at 3 P.M. tomorrow. There's nothing to be done about the larger problem but we can take measures to simplify the transition.* Frances gasped inwardly; the last word was a tactless violence against her.

The bouquet eclipsed Malcolm's head and shoulders. His voice came from behind the flowers: "What does it say?"

"Nothing," Frances said.

"Who's it from?"

"Nobody, nothing."

The elevator arrived and Frances pressed the penthouse button. Once in motion, she sought out the card in the bouquet. It was from the hostess of last night's party; Frances read it aloud: "'How lovely it was to peer across the room and to see you standing there, with your son, and your cigarette. I'm rich in friends but not so that I can't identify the gem of the bunch. Yours admiringly and ever fondly.'"

Frances had no immediate reaction or comment to these words, but in entering the apartment she relieved Malcolm of the bouquet, carried it to the kitchen, and jammed it into the garbage chute. Between the unkind honesty of the couriered letter and the abject stupidity of the card, she was beyond comfort.

Sometimes the world corrected itself, she knew this, for it had so many times in her past. She understood intuitively that it would not correct itself now, though.

# 3.

She ate breakfast at lunch in the library. Franklin Price, deceased nearly twenty years, had amassed a sizable collection of leather-bound first editions—an homage to a youthful fling with late-nineteenth-century literature. He had rarely cracked the books' pages, and Frances never had, but she enjoyed the room for its scent, and the sense of impenetrability the wall of books gave her. Malcolm entered the room. He hadn't changed out of his suit and his bloodshot eyes were hidden behind sunglasses. The maid brought him his breakfast and he ate it. Frances pushed her plate toward him and he began eating her remnants. She studied her son with a melancholic endearment.

"Did you drink to the brink of sound reasoning?"

"No."

"Were you driven to insomnia by the violence of your muse?"

He shook his head.

She laid a conciliatory hand atop his. "Menstruating?"

He winced, and she made a chaste face. She understood what was wrong with Malcolm. "How *are* things with Susan?" she asked.

"We're in our holding pattern, as if you didn't know."

"Oh, to be youngish and in love—ish." She took a drag from her cigarette. "When will you see her again?"

"We're having lunch today, actually." This was untrue, but he wanted to defend himself against her needling.

Frances masked her displeasure as best she could. In a pinched voice, she said, "I'd thought you were on the wane. Where will you eat?"

"I'm not sure yet."

Even if the lunch plan were a reality, he would have said the same thing, since it wasn't uncommon for Frances to interrupt his dates with Susan. "Is there room for me here?" she'd say after sitting down, the waiter already fawning at her side. Frances was a virtuosic manipulator of waiters; presently she would bring him in on some teasing game against Susan, a seemingly benign taunt relating to her ordering gazpacho out of season, or wearing her hat indoors. "It's an indoor hat," Susan would say—but she would remove it, face flushed, and another loss would be chalked up to the tally. Malcolm would do nothing to defend her, and the waiter wouldn't understand he was helping to trample Susan's spirit. Frances would insist on paying the bill.

"Well, I couldn't join you anyway," she told Malcolm. "I can't put Mr. Baker off another minute."

"What's he so excited about? Another plea for thrift?"

"Wait and see," Frances answered, and then became remote, sitting in silence, head side-cocked. Malcolm drifted from the library and to his room. He sat on the bed and watched the phone. It rang and he answered. Susan spoke in an unnaturally deep voice:

"Is your refrigerator running?"

"Hi, Sudsy. Did the cat drag you in?"

"Just now it did, yes. Will you come eat lunch with me?"

"Okay," he said. Then: "Wait, I'm sorry, I just ate."

Susan was quiet.

"I'll watch you eat," Malcolm volunteered.

"Every girl's dream," she said.

They met in a midtown bistro. Malcolm was late, Susan early. She sat alone in the booth, staring out the window. She hadn't been sleeping or eating and looked poorly, or what passed for poorly for her. She felt very dramatic in the moment, waiting for the object of her desire, the source of her pain. A rainstorm reared up and the citizens of New York dashed here and there to avoid the worst of it. Through the crowd came Malcolm, a slow-walking, solitary figure. He still hadn't changed his clothes, he had not shaved, he held no umbrella but appeared unconcerned at the fact of his being wet to the skin. His coat was unbuttoned and his bare, ample belly pressed against the see-through dress shirt. It seemed to Susan that each time they met he'd gained five pounds. He entered the restaurant and sat opposite Susan, rainwater dripping from his nose and hair. She removed his sunglasses and folded them onto the table.

"You look awful."

He held up a spoon and studied his reflection. "I've got a certain something." The waiter appeared and Malcolm, still watching himself, said, "Coffee and a short Scotch."

"Can I bring you anything to eat, sir?"

"I'll eat the Scotch."

The waiter went away. Malcolm lowered the spoon and Susan reached over, pinching his cheek.

"You know she's getting you fat on purpose, don't you?"

"I know."

"Do you think it's meant to turn me off specifically, or women in general?"

"You specifically. Women in general never cared for me." Malcolm took his stomach in his hands and sternly slapped it. "Is it working?"

"I preferred you before. But no, not really."

Susan's eyes were the color of honey; it hurt Malcolm to look at them, so he didn't. She watched him disappearing in his seat and wished to hit him, kiss him.

Soon the waiter brought the coffee, Scotch, and a towel for Malcolm to dry himself with. Malcolm drained the Scotch and began patting his hair with the towel.

"I've decided to try a new tack with you," Susan told him. "Would you like to hear what it is?"

"You can't scare me with a good time," Malcolm answered, wrapping the towel around his neck.

"Well, normally I ask a series of roundabout questions, approaching the subject, namely you, from seemingly unrelated angles. The answers, taken together, form a portrait of what's going on in that mausoleum you call a life."

"Right."

"I'm not going to do that anymore."

"Aren't you?"

"I'm going to interrogate you directly."

"I'm ready," he said, pouring cream into his coffee.

Susan folded her hands. "Has anything changed in regard to your relationship with your mother?"

"No."

"Do you have any reason to believe it will change within the span of the year?"

"No."

"Have you told her about our engagement?"

"No."

"Are you going to tell her?"

"I'd be surprised if I did."

"Have you thought any more about moving out?"

"I've thought about it."

"But will you do it?"

"I doubt it."

She took a moment. "The thing I can't figure out is whether or not you expect me, or if you even *want* me, to wait for you."

"Of course I want you to." Malcolm slurped his coffee. "But it wouldn't be very chivalrous to ask, would it?"

"And chivalry—is that an interest of yours?"

He laid the towel fully over his head. "I have many interests."

"Would you describe yourself as a coward?"

"No."

"How would you describe yourself?"

"I don't know that I'd bother in the first place."

She pulled the towel away from Malcolm's head and studied his olive-colored, unlined face. How had she come to care for this lugubrious toddler of a man? Love seemed evil at times, and human nature, this need to attain the unattainable, was so banal. Susan folded the towel on the table and said, "I want you to know that I am trying to fall out of love with you."

Malcolm's mouth creaked open, and he put his sunglasses back on. His silence conveyed pain, and Susan was pleased her words had had an effect. Still, she knew she had achieved nothing, and that victory was as far off as ever. She'd often wondered what Frances would do if she were in her position; now she asked Malcolm and he stirred, speaking as though he'd worked the question through long ago: "She'd never have found herself in your position in the first place."

It was always this way. No matter what she said to wound him, the simple facts hurt her more. Frances would never let go of Malcolm, Susan knew this. She asked Malcolm to leave her alone and he stood to go. "I'm going to kiss your forehead," he said warningly, then he did, and exited the restaurant, forgetting to pay for his Scotch and coffee.

Susan resumed her window gazing. The rain had stopped, replaced by radiant sunshine. Minutes had passed when she noticed Malcolm was standing across the street, watching her. His sunglasses were crooked; steam was rising from his damp shoulders. He was a pile of American garbage and she feared she would love him forever.

# 4.

Mr. Baker was a mouselike man, which isn't to say he behaved as one, but that he truly did look very much like a mouse. Sometimes he looked like an angry mouse, sometimes wise; on this day, as he sat waiting for Frances to arrive, he resembled a mouse who wished he were another mouse. He had been enamored of Franklin Price; coming up the ranks he'd had the honor of witnessing the great litigator in court any number of times. The first case was still clear in his memory—a minor affair, a hostile takeover of some Midwestern communications company, but Mr. Baker had never seen Price's equal for controlled brutality and pure showmanship. It was on this day that Mr. Baker grasped the elusive point: the court was a performance environment, a stage play whereby the actors conceived their lines on the spot, and it was the finest entertainer who won the prize. From the instant Price rose from his chair to speak, all in the courtroom were rapt. Restrained applause followed his closing arguments. Mr. Baker afterward followed Price's career with an almost fanatical fervor.

Price personified all that Mr. Baker held to be of any importance. Certainly he looked the part: he was a dashing man, poised, stylishly attired; but this was offset by the needed amount of menace, a tactile pulse of psychic violence. It was difficult to speak with Price because if you bored him, he told you you did; and if you bothered him, there was in his carriage and language a hostility that one could not help but equate with actual bloodshed. Price was never recognized for physical mayhem, but his dismissals were just the same as a wallop in the face.

For all the inhabitants of this particular landscape, there was the pursuit of money as a primary, as *the* primary goal. This was key to Price, of course, and in the years making up the first half of his career he accrued a legitimate if modest fortune. But there were others who made more, which must have displeased him, for he set out to address this during the second half of his career, the phase that came to define him.

Price became known as the most vicious, the most tenacious litigator, defending only the indefensible: the tobacco and pharmaceutical industries, the apparatus of the war machine, gun lobbyists. Mr. Baker was not above the occasional unsavory pursuit, particularly if the pay was sound, but Price took one repugnant case after another, with never a break in between, so that his own persona became indivisible from that of those he worked for. The collective assumption was that he enjoyed his role in the wrongdoing. Whether or not this was the truth, who could say; what was indisputable was Price's prosperity. He was among the highest-paid lawyers in the United States, and his every extracurricular investment was seemingly predetermined to turn a profit. Sensible, professional men and women spoke with sober seriousness of Franklin Price as one imbued with and directed by dark energies. Up-and-comers shared a joke, which was to discreetly genuflect when they crossed Price's path.

His death came unexpectedly, while the man was at his zenith, and was thrilling in its details. The coroner who performed the autopsy said he'd never seen so powerful a heart attack in his long years at practice, and his line, often repeated by Price's cronies and enemies, was that the overtaxed organ had *exploded like a goddamned hand grenade.* The fact of his wife's discovering his body, then going skiing in Vail for the weekend without bothering to call the authorities, was somehow fitting as an ending, the just debasement of a man who in all honesty had it coming. The tabloids ran a photograph of Frances attending an après-ski party at the mountain lodge, and she had never looked more glamorous or pleased; the image presented her to the public as one reveling in the private knowledge of the stiffening corpse of her husband. The picture in question was five years old but the tabloids couldn't see the point in stating that, and so they didn't.

The hushed discussions in the following years that Frances, that witty, fearful beauty, had gone quietly mad and now addressed her aged cat as Price represented a weird icing on an already weird cake. It was a good story, and so it was told, and told again, and it brought a reliable delight to the tellers and audience both.

Mr. Baker had seen no evidence of this particular mania in Frances. All he knew was that anyone who could hold her own against the formidable Franklin Price—and by all accounts

Frances did more than hold her own—was one deserving of his respect, and from the start of their working together he had afforded her this. She'd received it as a matter of course, and for the first years of their collaboration had extended him a mirrored respect along with the occasional small kindness. But as time passed, and the estate faltered, Mr. Baker had become for her a totem of disintegration, and she turned away from the man. So began their game of go-seek.

Having made every effort to salvage her holdings, Mr. Baker suffered no professional guilt: Frances's spending was pathological. How many times had he reached out to beg for frugality, only to learn later that the warning had kicked off a frenzy of lavish purchases? She bought homes in cities she never intended to visit; she gave staggering sums to charities whose aim she could not accurately name. Mr. Baker couldn't rid himself of the notion that ruin was the object of the game for Frances. But was she herself aware of it? That is, was she perhaps attempting to distance herself from what could be considered dirty money? For what his opinion was worth, he thought her motivation was not linked to morality, but something smaller, something more personal, and bitterer.

He'd experienced a queasiness in the recent months whenever her name came to mind, knowing the matter was beyond hope, and knowing he would eventually have to have the conversation he most dreaded having with his clients. He was having that conversation now. Before Frances had settled in her chair, Mr. Baker spoke:

"It's all gone, Frances."

"What's all gone?"

"Everything."

Frances took a drink of water. "Everything," she said.

"Yes."

"Not the money in my account."

"It's not your account for long."

"It's in my name."

"The name you get to keep. But every penny in that account, in addition to the investments and properties, is going back to the bank."

Frances said, "The properties."

"The properties are yours I would imagine until the end of the month. By that I mean you have use of them. But they can none of them be sold or rented, and you will be locked out on the first of January at the latest."

Frances took another sip of water, then held the cool glass to her cheek. "Certainly I'll get to keep the money I brought to the marriage?"

"That was shuffled into the estate a long time ago and it was not, excuse me, a very large sum."

"What about Malcolm's legacy?"

"No," said Mr. Baker.

"What are we meant to live off once the bank has moved against us?"

"I can't claim to know the answer to that." It was grotesque to see a person such as Frances exposed in this way, and Mr. Baker was peeved to be party to it. He told her, "I spoke to you about this as a possibility for seven years, and as an eventuality for three. What did you think was going to happen? What was your plan?"

She exhaled. "My plan was to die before the money ran out. But I kept and keep not dying, and here I am." She shook her head at herself, then sat up. "All right, then. It's all been settled, and now I want you to tell me what to do."

"Do," he said.

"Yes. Tell me, please."

"What else is there to do but start over?"

"And what does that mean, I wonder? When you know I've never generated money, but only spent it?"

"What can I say, Frances? Take a loan from a friend?"

"Impossible. Name something else."

"There is nothing else."

"There is something else."

Mr. Baker looked away and back. He said, "Speaking off the record, there's only one thing you can do: sell it all."

"Sell what all?"

"Everything that isn't nailed down. Sell the jewelry, the art, the books. Sell it privately, quietly, cheaply. Bring me the checks and I'll transfer it to cash for you."

"And then what?"

"And then whatever-you-wish."

"But where will we live?"

"I suppose you'll have to rent."

To hear the word, it was like swallowing a sharp crust of stale bread, and Frances winced. No one was going to help her, she realized, and she felt very small and cold. She stood. Staring at Mr. Baker's forehead she said, "Thank you for everything. I don't suppose we'll be seeing each other again."

"Frances, sit," he said. "Order some lunch."

"I need to breathe."

"It's not a death."

"I need to leave."

That evening, Malcolm came into the kitchen to find Frances sharpening a long, gleaming knife at the marble-top island. She worked with a sense of rhythm, and intently. Malcolm had never seen her perform this or any other kitchen duty before, and he asked her, "Are you *cooking?*"

"No, I only like the sound it makes," she said, lightly panting, the vein on her forehead plumped. "How was your time with Susan?"

Malcolm murmured indistinctly.

"What's that, Mr. Mumbles? I can't understand you. Well, my news trumps yours. Are you ready for this? We're insolvent. We've nothing left. Nothing in the world!" She laughed dementedly, cutting at the air with the knife. It came away from her hand, clattering down the length of the island and onto the floor. Malcolm was unnerved, and went away from her. Alone again, Frances collected the knife and resumed her work of sharpening the blade, but more slowly than before.

# 5.

There came a busy phase. Mr. Baker put Frances in touch with a man named Ralph Rudy, who would act as the go-between in charge of liquidating the remnants of the estate. "His pedigree is murky, but he's hungry, and he knows his stuff," Mr. Baker said. "Stay out of his way, Frances. He'll do the work, all right."

Mr. Rudy did not exude prosperity. Also, he was not friendly. During the tour of the house he spoke almost not at all and was disinterested in Frances's descriptions of her possessions, the anecdotes surrounding their purchase. He scratched out his notes in a warped spiral pad with a pencil stub so small it was not visible in his fleshy hand. He made a show of shielding the notes from Frances, who, unaccustomed to indignity of any kind, experienced a sort of emotional vertigo, a loathsome chill running down her arms and to the tips of her fingers. After the tour they sat in the kitchen.

"Do you understand the nature of my situation?" she asked. "The delicacy of it, I mean?"

Mr. Rudy nodded. He had no thought to put Frances at ease. "My fee," he said.

"Yes?" said Frances.

"It's a straight thirty percent. And that's nonnegotiable."

"Isn't it?"

"No."

"Mightn't it be? Well, it's going to have to be if you want to work with me."

Ralph Rudy flinched. He hadn't looked Frances in the eye until now; in doing so he recognized his underestimation. She recognized his recognition, her expression explaining, *You are a bland, stupid man, and I will give you no quarter.* "Twenty-seven percent," he found himself saying.

"I will give you fifteen percent or I'll thank you for your time."

"Twenty-five percent."

Frances clasped her hands together. Now came the moment she most appreciated. She said, "If you name another figure that is not fifteen percent, I will go to fourteen percent. Name another, I go to thirteen, and on down the line until your payment, and your sole function in regard to my own life, disappears altogether."

Mr. Rudy scowled. "That's no way to negotiate."

"It's the only way."

"This is a tricky job. There's a risk you're not accounting for."

"The risk is my own."

"But this could be detrimental to my reputation."

"Reputation." Frances smiled. "That's humorous."

"Is that right?"

"Yes, it is."

"And why?"

"Because," she said, "I saw the state of your rattling vehicle

when you pulled up. Because the vehicle wore New Jersey li-
cense plates. Because your socks, while coming close, don't quite
match. Because a cursory investigation turned up that you were
recently fired from Sotheby's for blatant misrepresentation and
only narrowly avoided going to prison for this. And because,
and because, and because. There's no need for us to insult each
other, Mr. Rudy. I have a somewhat dirty job that needs doing,
and you are a somewhat dirty person. You seem to think you
have me over a barrel, but I've other options you're not taking
into consideration."

"There's no one in North America with my contacts,"
Mr. Rudy said sharply.

"I don't doubt that. But you miss my point." She looked
away, over his head. "Have you heard any rumors with respect
to my mental health?"

"No." He paused. "I've heard you're odd."

"Odd."

"Odd, yes. Difficult."

"Difficult."

Mr. Rudy cleared his throat. "There's the story of your husband, too."

Frances looked confused. "I'm sorry, which story is that?"
she asked.

"You know. About you finding him."

"Yes?" she said.

"You *know*," Mr. Rudy said. He was uncomfortable.

Frances raised a finger, as though she'd stumbled across
the answer herself. "I found him, but then I left him awhile,
didn't I?"

Mr. Rudy nodded.

"And people *still* talk about that?" asked Frances amusedly.

"Sure they do. I mean, you know. Of course."

Frances shook her head. She leaned in, close enough that Mr. Rudy felt her breath on his face as she spoke: "I'm going to tell you a private truth, now: I'm *more* than odd. There's a goodly part of me that wants to set this building afire, with myself and my son locked in. What do you think of that?"

Mr. Rudy appeared adrift. "That's none of my business."

"I say it is. Because if I don't get my price, this goodly part may well become ever more goodly. It's important, Mr. Rudy, that you understand my point of view, and appreciate both the fact and scope of my nihilism. Now, you and I know that many of the objects in this house are of an uncommon quality. My effects represent a small fortune. Fifteen percent of that, even in a hushed, rushed sale? Think of how many socks that would buy." Mr. Rudy's eyelids dropped, and he became pensive. Frances said, "Now let's walk together, not speaking, to the front door."

They did this, shaking hands in the vestibule, and Mr. Rudy surprised himself by agreeing to the 15 percent commission. He knew he should dislike this woman, but he didn't or couldn't. As a man who disliked most everyone, himself especially, it was an exotic, heady feeling. "Call me Ralph," he said.

"I will call you Mr. Rudy."

She shut the door in his face and retired to the library, ringing the maid for an old-fashioned. The winter sun was radiant in the windows and her blood thrilled at life's gruesome pageant. She rang Malcolm's room; he answered but didn't speak, he only sat there breathing. "Come on down, pal," she said. "Let's consider the bright sides together." She hung up the phone and drank and waited.

# 6.

Liquidation under way, Frances and Malcolm returned to their suites at the Four Seasons. They saw nothing of each other during this time.

Malcolm read. His momentary focus of study was the memoir recollections of disastrous voyages into uninhabitable regions of the world. He lived in his robe, with curtains drawn, the television on but muted. He never changed the channel; it was something he would glance at from time to time, as one looking out the window to check the weather. He ordered six full meals per day: breakfasts at nine and eleven; lunches at two and four; and dinners at seven and eleven. He was eating not with anger, not with desperation or sorrow, but with rigor, as though this gorging were part of a strict training. In the afternoon he pulled on his trunks and visited the pool but otherwise he never left his room. By the fourth day he couldn't manage the small talk that came with receiving his meals, and so he had them left outside his door. He knew from experience that he was suffering from the hotel unwellness.

Frances became involved with a number of reality-based TV shows. Anything having to do with incarceration and she was helpless to look away. The clang of a prison gate, the echoing, menacing chatter of distant unseen inmates, the rattle of keys on a polyester-clad guard: it was catnip for Frances. It wasn't that she relished the misfortune of others, or that she took solace in her own freedom. She and Malcolm both were moved, in their respective areas of interest, by a sheer experience described in such detail that it achieved palpability. They were drinking steadily, if not heavily.

Joan was often in touch with Frances, sending notes and leaving messages with the concierge. Frances had been avoiding Joan but increasingly she wished to unburden herself. They met for brunch one Sunday morning in early December.

"Are they saying I'm broke?"

"They are." Joan chomped a piece of celery. "Are you? Talk to old Joan."

"I am."

"And what does the word mean: broke?"

"It means that I have nothing."

"And when you say: nothing?"

Frances explained. Joan listened with perfect seriousness. "And what," she said, "what if I were to bring up the topic of a loan?"

"Oh, but you mustn't do that."

"What about a gift? Would that be better, or worse?"

"Either one would be the same ugly thing."

"Won't you please bend on this?"

"No."

Joan said, "A plan is coming to me."

Frances waited, watching.

"Possibly it's idiotic," Joan continued. "But it's an option, and the more of those you have the better, isn't that right?"

Frances waited still.

"My Paris apartment. I haven't been in, what, a year and a half? And it's just sitting there."

Frances was nodding. She understood the proposition, and was wondering whether or not to bother hiding her shame. Joan took up her friend's hand. "Don't rush to think of it in any one light, darling. It's only sensible."

"Sensible," said Frances.

"Sensible."

"Sensible." Frances was experiencing the phenomenon of a familiar word losing its meaning. "Sensible."

Joan felt outraged; she pinched Frances's arm, hard. Frances mouthed an *Ow!* but made no sound. She rapped the top of Joan's hand with the scoop of her spoon. "Ow!" said Joan, and they sat back in their chairs, Frances rubbing her arm, Joan her hand, each watching the other with a sober expression.

The waiter appeared and they ordered their lunch and a bottle of wine. They ate their lunch and drank their wine and then came a second bottle, which they also drank. Paris was not decided, but it began to look rosier, for it was viable, and as a plan it possessed at least a measure of style. They spoke of the city in youthful, romantic terms. They'd both been in love, and both had been loved in Paris, France. Joan expressed jealousy at the thought of Frances's moving there permanently or semi-permanently and Frances accepted this at the start, but when it went on too long she said it was beneath them, this banter, and that they should approach the event for what it was.

"Which is what?" said Joan. "What are we calling it?"

"Annihilation."

The waiter appeared. "How was everything today, ladies?"

"Perfection."

When the check came, Frances and Joan reached for it simultaneously. There was a seated tussle and the bill soon was ripped to pieces by their clawing hands, the both of them trilling with laughter. The waiter brought them a new bill and Frances ceremoniously passed it to Joan. They were holding hands as they exited the restaurant, and Frances looked to be near tears. Later, smoking in the alley, the waiter was made contemplative by the memory of her. Her beauty had not been diminished by her sadness; he had held his breath as he watched her move from his sight line.

She said goodbye to Joan and returned to her home to find it empty. The staff had been let go, but Mr. Rudy was pacing the property and clucking with self-satisfaction. He'd made many shrewd sales, and so Frances sought to endure his attitude; but then he began acting strangely, calling her Francey, touching her bare wrist. He was wearing a new suit and an abundant, musky scent. When he suggested they celebrate their successes over dinner, she laid a cool hand upon his ample face and said, "Mr. Rudy, I'd sooner fuck an eel." After this he affected a high-road attitude, which she also endured. As they went over the figures she felt certain he'd massaged the payout in his favor but she didn't pursue it, she merely took her cut with thanks and sent him on his oily way. The check denoted a fair amount, but not enough to represent anything besides a provisional pardon, and she studied the zeroes with a sadness that felt treacherous. She couriered the check to Mr. Baker and asked him to have the funds transferred to euros as quickly as he was able.

# 7.

Malcolm was yet in his suite. He was speaking to Susan on the phone.

"Let's eat food, for lunch," she said.

"Can't do that."

"Let's drink a drink in a bar."

"No."

Recalling certain past behaviors, she deduced he was in the grips of the hotel unwellness. In a patient tone, she said, "I want to see you, Malcolm. Tell me, how should I achieve this?"

"I think I could swim," he said.

Ninety minutes later he was standing beside the pool in trunks, while Susan trod water before him. He crouched into a squatting ball, toes hanging over the pool's edge. Tipping slowly forward, he flopped into the water. His body rose to the surface, facedown, lifeless. A long while passed; Susan watched, smiling. They had swum together many times and she expected a performance. Malcolm breached, gasping. "We called that one Dead Man's Float," he said.

"Who's 'we'?"

"My school friends and I."

"You never had a friend."

"I had four friends."

"What were they like?"

"Rich brats, like me. One was sex obsessed, one was sporty, one was gay, I guess. One was weirdly content."

"Who were you?"

He wondered how he should put it. "A lump of heartbroken clay."

"Why were you heartbroken?"

"Well," he said. "It was before Frances came around. I've told you all this."

"Not really you haven't." They were facing each other, swimming in place. "Tell me now," she said.

He took in a mouthful of water and spit it upward in a thick stream. "Who knows where to start."

"Start at the end."

"My father died and Frances showed up unannounced at the academy."

"And you didn't know her very well at this point, right?"

"Hardly."

"Had you known your father?"

"Almost not at all."

"But you were heartbroken about his dying?"

"No, I was ashamed of that."

"Because of the way it happened," she said.

"Of course. It was in all the papers, you know. Fragrant

Frank Price. My father had made so many enemies, and they were having a lot of fun with the details. And my mother was made out to be some sort of monster."

"Did the other kids know about it?"

"Yes."

"And were they terrible?"

"Yes."

A moment passed. Susan said, "Tell me why you were heartbroken, Malcolm."

"I was heartbroken because Frances and my father never made the pretense of having even a passing interest in me. Most of us at the academy felt this to one degree or another but my parents were extreme. Not a word on my birthday. Not a card. Ten months had passed without my seeing either one of them, then my father died and Frances showed up in a fur coat, tipsy at eleven o'clock in the morning. 'How are you, pal?' she asked me."

"Were you angry with her?"

"I was in awe of her."

"And she took you away from the academy."

"She asked me what I wanted to do and I said I didn't know. She said, 'Do you want to come away with me?' and I said that I did."

"How old were you?"

"Twelve years old."

Susan's arms were starting to burn but she continued swimming. There was no one around but them; the air was warm, the pool cool, the light dim, and all sounds were softened, doubled. Malcolm's face had gone blank. It was rumored that after Frances took him out of school he'd never gone back, and she asked him if this was true.

"I never set foot in a classroom again," he said. "But, there was Ms. Mackey."

Ms. Mackey was Malcolm's tutor. She came to the apartment each weekday for two years. In the beginning she taught him French; here was the reason Frances had hired her. Once this was accomplished, Frances did not dismiss her but asked that she stay and teach Malcolm "other things." She asked Frances what this meant and Frances replied, "Things that are fascinating." Ms. Mackey took this to mean she could teach Malcolm whatever she wished, and she did this.

She was a slender, melancholic woman of thirty-five with a gap in her front teeth and aching, pale blue eyes. Certain of their days were devoted to her unanswerable auto-queries relating to the mean stupidity of existence, the fallibility of romantic love, her suspicion that dissatisfaction and shortcoming were constants of the human condition. Once she said, "I keep trying to march in time but the drummer's out to get me." Occasionally she would fail to show up and Malcolm would call her at home. Her explanations ran to naked admissions; she was bowing to pressures larger than she could address. "But tomorrow I'll be there, Malcolm, I promise. Are you missing me very much? I like it when you sit there scratching your belly at me, you little gentleman." By the end of their first year together Malcolm was in love with her, and she knew it, and treated his love with care and caution. She was pleased to wield this power over him but she neither abused it nor cultivated it.

They worked mornings in the library, then would eat lunch together in a restaurant or café. Frances wanted Malcolm to eat out daily because, as she told Ms. Mackey, "Waiters know more about life than anyone else in the world." Malcolm felt grand when they dined; he began to settle the bills himself and he respected currency for the role it allowed him. If a waiter flirted with Ms. Mackey, Malcolm would not tip him a penny. If he treated Malcolm as an equal, the man was richly rewarded. Ms. Mackey lamented this behavior, pointing out that money was too often used in lieu of verbal communication. But she couldn't deny that she was charmed by Malcolm, and she told him as much.

On his fourteenth birthday, Ms. Mackey did not arrive for their lessons, didn't answer his calls or return his messages. The next day it was the same, and in the afternoon he took the subway, for the first time in his life, to her apartment. Malcolm described the scenario to Susan: "She answered the door in a robe with a stain down the front. She seemed scared; she pulled me in like I was late to meet her. Her apartment was dismal: a mattress on the floor, bedsheet tacked to the window, and her fridge was leaking water across the kitchen. The realization that she was poor was very shocking to me. I hadn't seen anything like that before, and I was actually frightened by it. She was speaking English; she wouldn't respond to me in French. She sat me down and asked, strangely cheery, 'What can I do for you?'

"'It's my birthday,' I told her.

"'Your birthday was yesterday.'

"It was painful that she'd known but hadn't reached out. I asked why she hadn't come and she politely said, 'I'm inside of something at the moment, Malcolm.'

"'When are you coming back?'

"She thought about it. 'Two days.'

"So, I went home and waited. Frances noticed I was alone

and asked where Ms. Mackey was. I said she was sick but that she'd be back soon. There must have been too much emotion in my response; Frances smelled a rat and started interrogating me. Pretty soon she had me admitting Ms. Mackey was my heart's desire. I felt like I was sharing good news but when I finished, Frances called Ms. Mackey and fired her. I never saw her again. I was devastated but it took me a month to work up the courage to go back to her apartment. The super said she'd moved, he didn't know where. Frances asked me if I wanted to go back to school and I said I didn't and she said that that was fine, but that I'd need to spend regular time in museums and libraries."

"What's 'regular time' mean?" said Susan.

"Five hours a day, five days a week. The Met, the Cloisters, the Frick, the Morgan Library. Place to place to place."

"For how long?"

"Four years."

Susan said, "You went to museums, alone, five hours a day, five days a week, for four years?"

"Yes."

"Weren't you lonely?"

"I was lonely."

"Frances never went with you?"

"Almost never. I wanted her to. Once she said, 'What if they decide I'm a sculpture, and won't let me come home?'" He smiled at the memory, then pushed off the wall of the pool and began swimming lazy, crooked laps.

Susan thought of the time they'd met. It was during a gully in her life; she'd finished school and was home, wondering at the nullity before her and acquainting herself with a creeping sense of lack, chiefly in the area of love. Men had always chased after Susan, and she found the attention pleasing but ultimately unfulfilling. And it was stifling, as her suitors, at the slightest reciprocation, were so quick to assume ownership of her. She did not love these people. She had known something like love during the final year of her studies but it was oversimple, both the man, named Tom, and his plan. His speedy acceptance of her as his lifelong mate was suspicious; he selected her as if off a rack. She tried to think of him as decisive as opposed to robotic, but failed, and she could never achieve a deeper admiration for him. She broke off the engagement in the moments preceding the graduation ceremony. Tom's face as he crossed the stage to accept his diploma expressed a whole contempt, and just afterward he spoke to her in a bellow over the cacophony of screaming students surrounding them: "I know it's boring and I should probably just suck it up but I want you to know you're a definite shithead." Graduation caps swooped through the air like bats; Susan watched from behind oversized sunglasses.

She'd been home a number of weeks and was sulking in her parents' bedroom, avoiding the cocktail party downstairs, when Malcolm emerged from her dead father's closet winding a wristwatch. When she cleared her throat, he flinched, wearing the face of a man caught out. She approached and asked if he was, as it appeared, stealing her father's watch. He admitted he was, then asked her on a date. She said she was thinking of screaming; he told her to hold her horses and she did hold them. Malcolm assured Susan that if she ate with him they would have a conversation of some interest, and that he would return the watch at meal's end, and perhaps they could forge a friendship into the bargain. She knew better than to go along with it but she was, as stated, unexcited by the cocktail party; and beyond that, she knew just to look in Malcolm's eyes that he hadn't an evil thought in his head, and was no more dangerous than a walk in the park.

They lunched. Halfway through the meal she realized he was the son of the deceased Franklin Price, and now his already intriguing persona was doused in scandal. After he paid the bill she requested that he return the watch. "Oh, please, Susan, can I keep it," he said softly. She was endeared by his solemn desire, but admitted he was making her uncomfortable.

"I'm uncomfortable almost all of the time," he confessed.

"Do you know that my father is dead?"

"I didn't. Were you close with him?"

"Not very close."

"Did you hate him?"

"No."

"But you didn't love him, either, did you?"

"He was my father," she answered.

He relaxed in his chair and shut his eyes, as though sunning. "It's good, when fathers die," he said, pressing the watch to his ear.

Susan was smiling but wasn't sure why. "I might let you borrow it," she said.

"Ah-ha," said Malcolm.

Their relationship was initially platonic. They went to the movies. Malcolm loved the movies, all movies, even badly written, directed, and acted ones. Actually he seemed to have no opinion of any one film he saw; he would only say afterward, "I love going to the movies." He would not speak nor field a word the moment the lights dimmed. When the film was over, they walked, hours-long strolls in all manner of weather with no destination, and Malcolm spoke easily, though not of anything particularly revealing.

He described himself as an avid swimmer but Susan found he did not swim so much as float; he did not wish to exercise, but to experience submersion and wetness.

He drank, at times to excess, but there was nothing dark about it; he was looking not to kill a thought but to reset the clock, to force an occurrence. He called her one morning after a late night, and though obviously in great physical pain he spoke with earnest regard of the unassailable justice of the hangover. She'd not met anyone like him before and she admired him for his uncommon, complicated, almost entirely untenable belief systems. He never said a dull word, she learned, and he summoned in her a curiosity that her usual friends never had.

But did she introduce him into her circle? The thought was impossible. Malcolm was unafraid of social discomfort, which is not to say that he courted it; but it was common enough that he assumed it requisite, and endured it without grievance. As his position in her life became more prominent, Susan imagined the disastrous collision of worlds: Her girlfriends happening upon her and Malcolm in a restaurant, and insisting they all eat together. Malcolm would not remove his sunglasses. He would order his eggs "really loosely scrambled," then drown them in tomato juice. He would not speak unless spoken to and then only briefly, and a frost would take the group, an agonizing silence. The worst part of this scenario was the thought of the discussion that would transpire once Susan and Malcolm had gone. There would be shrieking, Susan knew. She endeavored to avoid the scenario at all costs.

Malcolm was unaware of Susan's concerns. He had no room in his mind for thoughts of her life beyond the time they shared together, and so he could never be offended by her refusal to bring him around to meet her peers.

Susan thought of Malcolm as an exotic pet, a stopgap antidote to postcollege doldrums, but then something terrible happened, which was that she fell in love with him. It was like an illness coming on; it loitered at the edges of her consciousness, then pounced, gripping her mind and heart. She thought it must be temporary, and waited some days before addressing it, when all at once she couldn't bear to keep quiet.

They were sitting on the Great Lawn in Central Park. Malcolm was pointing to a hummingbird hovering above them. The bird performed an oblong circle, and again, then paused, shot away. Malcolm had followed these actions with the tip of his finger. He was pointing at an empty sky when Susan told him, "Well, Malcolm, I'm sorry to break up the party but it looks like I'm in love with you." He removed a cheese sandwich he'd been secretly carrying in his jacket pocket and ate this in silence. After, they moved through the park. She reached for him, clamping her fingers awkwardly around his wrist. He stopped walking and laced their fingers together.

"This is how we're going to hold hands," he told her.

Malcolm did not not mention Frances, but there was a resistance to Frances-as-topic. Susan repressed alarm when she realized Malcolm and his mother still lived together; and though he spoke of her as one in need of assistance, the volume of their activities contradicted this. When she called him to meet, as often as not he said he was busy. Busy doing what? "I'd like to meet your friends, someday," she told him. "Oh, I don't have any friends," he replied. There was no remorse in this. It was stated the way someone else might have said, "I don't have a car." Further investigation brought the situation with Frances into sharper focus. Susan was made uneasy by the timbre of Malcolm's voice when the subject of his mother arose. He was so plainly and relentlessly smitten with the woman, it was impossible for Susan not to view Frances as antagonistic to her happiness. "I want to meet your mother," she finally told Malcolm, who winced and hissed and drank his drink. Frances was *difficult*, he said; she could be *meddlesome*. But these warnings, along with Frances's infamously bizarre behavior following the death of Malcolm's father, served only to entice Susan. One and a half years into their relationship, and in the wake of dogged badgering, Malcolm resignedly organized a dinner for the three of them at his and Frances's home.

Susan arrived at the appointed time, fist poised to knock when Frances opened the door. In her youth she had been renowned for her beauty and style, and these attributes were still in evidence, but she had a searching, malevolent flicker in her eye that marred her person and kept Susan at a remove. Frances told her, "Stand up straight and let's see what you are." Susan already was standing up straight, however. Actually it seemed most everything Frances said to Susan that night was, upon consideration, an insult. "Was it a gift?" she asked about an admittedly daring bracelet Susan wore. And when Susan didn't lick her plate clean, Frances commented, "I'm too old to even *think* of dieting."

Martinis were served in the library after dinner. Frances sat across from Susan, drunk to the point of stillness. Occasionally she would look over at Susan and softly laugh, murmuring some bitter remark to herself. Then she began to stare. It was just the same way a leopard might peer out at spectators in a zoo, the eyes explaining, *If it weren't for this pane of glass I would eat you up.* Malcolm was a hologram that night, granting Susan nothing but the occasional partly sympathetic nod: *You asked for it*, he seemed to be saying, which was true, of course, and obnoxious.

The evening was a catastrophe, in short. When the pain of silence became acute, Susan stood and announced her departure. Malcolm was sleeping or pretending to sleep; Frances walked Susan out, caressing her hand, and demanding she return when she was feeling "more like herself." After Frances shut the door, Susan stood on the sidewalk staring up at the apartment. She was ill at ease to a degree that seemed outsize to what had occurred that night. An unknown voice spoke to Susan, and it said to her, *Be careful.* Frances appeared in the window; Susan walked away.

The mother of the man she had accidentally fallen in love with did not approve of their union: this was so. But it was a common problem, wasn't it? It was a trope. She quieted her instinct. It could never have occurred to her that Frances would actively try to dismantle their relationship, and furthermore, that she would succeed.

In the swimming pool at the Four Seasons, Susan learned Frances had done just this. Malcolm explained he was leaving for Paris. His departure was imminent and for all he knew permanent. Susan's numerous panicked questions were met with Malcolm at his vaguest and most maddening. The inquisition trailed off; there was nothing more to say; the time had come for Susan to give up once and for all. She felt struck. In a powdery voice she asked Malcolm, "Why don't you love me correctly?"

Possibly he heard; he didn't answer her. "The Sinking Sword," he said. Plunging underwater, he hung upside down. Raising his right leg ceiling-ward, toes rigid as a dancer en pointe, he exhaled. The hairless leg began its slow submersion, soon disappearing altogether, and there was nothing on the water's surface but a low, rolling boil.

# 8.

Malcolm and Frances breakfasted in her suite. They spoke of small things, and it was not evident to look at them that they were about to quit their lives. Frances asked Malcolm to check them out of the hotel and he attempted it but returned bearing news that each of his credit cards had been declined. Frances called down to speak with the concierge; when her request for a line of credit was denied, she grew irate: "Don't 'Mrs. Price' me, what's-your-name. How many hundreds of thousands of dollars of mine do you have?"

"I personally have none," said the concierge. "The hotel thanks you for your long patronage. We are looking forward to further mutually beneficial exchanges between us. Please let me know how we may assist you in reaching your current goal."

Frances hung up. Malcolm offered his remaining cash to settle the bill but she explained they were going to need it to buy their tickets out of the country. Frances arranged for their

copious baggage to be discreetly collected by a town car driver,
then she and Malcolm left the hotel without paying their bill,
returning on foot to their building. In the lobby, the doorman
informed them that a bank representative had put a lockbox on
the front door of their apartment. Frances and Malcolm drifted
back outside, where they discovered Small Frank sitting glumly
on the sidewalk. "Hello, asshole," said Frances. The cat looked at
her, then away. She told Malcolm she had an errand to run, and
for him to meet her at the passenger ship terminal on Twelfth
Avenue at noon. He walked away without a word, Small Frank
following behind; a moment later the town car pulled up. Frances tapped her watch. "I admire your timing," she told the driver.

"I admire your coat," the driver replied. He drove her to
Mr. Baker's offices in midtown. Mr. Baker's assistant was laying
out juice and pastries and Mr. Baker sat beaming in his chair,
behaving as though he and Frances had concluded a pleasant
piece of business together, and now he wished to discuss the
opportunities to come. He asked Frances why she'd needed the
money in euros and she told him, "I'm going to Paris."

"That's right, you talk the talk, don't you?"

"*Oui, petit cochon.*" Mr. Baker didn't understand. "Little
prince," she explained.

Her cash stood in neat stacks on the table between them.
Mr. Baker watched as she transferred the banded monies into
her large black shoulder bag. He knew he should say something,
decided he wouldn't, but then couldn't not.

"A hundred and seventy thousand euros loose in your
purse?"

She slid the bag over her shoulder. "You've never been boring before," she said. "Why start now?"

He stood, extending his hand. "I'm going to miss you, Frances."

"Yes, won't you all." She shook his hand and left. Mr. Baker turned to his assistant with a look of fond amusement on his face.

"They broke the mold with that one," he said.

"*Cochon* means 'pig,'" the assistant told him.

Malcolm and Small Frank were waiting outside the passenger ship terminal next to a dumpster exploded with trash. As the driver began unloading their luggage onto the sidewalk, Malcolm realized they would be taking a cruise ship to France. As one who suffered from seasickness, he asked her to reconsider air travel. Frances was apologetic but immovable: she was engaging her crisis in full dramatic tilt and wanted, needed to face the limitless ocean with a terrific, stabbing pain in her heart. She asked Malcolm for his cash and he passed it over.

They entered the terminal and followed the folding line to the ticket station. Frances purchased two first-class suites from a sad, gray man at a podium. "Passports," he said, and Frances handed these over. When the man noticed Small Frank cradled in Malcolm's arms, he requested documentation for the animal. Frances explained she had none and the man heaved a sigh of spiritual exhaustion. "I can't allow you to bring an undocumented animal on board the ship," he said.

"That's fine," said Frances, and she told Malcolm, "Put him outside, please." Malcolm moved to deposit Small Frank on the sidewalk in front of the terminal.

The man at the podium watched this in silent disbelief. When Malcolm returned, the man at the podium said, "You're just going to leave him on the sidewalk?"

"That's right," Frances answered.

"You're going to leave him on the sidewalk and go to France?"

"Paris, France."

The man at the podium shook his head. He was half-perusing their passports but a peevishness was growing in him. At last, he couldn't hold back. "You bring an animal into your life, you've got a responsibility to do right by that animal." Frances nudged the passports closer to the man. He was disgusted, but had no legal recourse to keep Frances and Malcolm from leaving the United States; he handed them their passports and tickets and curtly waved them on. Small Frank, meanwhile, had snuck back into the terminal and now was walking along the interior wall toward the point of embarkment.

Frances and Malcolm checked their baggage and made their way toward the looming vessel. Frances was excited by the sight and size of it, but Malcolm felt instantly queasy, mistrustful of his legs to carry him. It was a skyscraper laid on its side, larger than any seagoing vessel should ever be, he decided, and representing human ambition at its unsightliest. The check-in process took place at the top of the gangplank and Malcolm could not, he found, take part; he stood to the right of his mother, not daring to look anywhere other than directly at his own homely brown leather shoes, telling himself to *breathe, breathe, keep breathing.* His stomach was squirming by the time he arrived at his suite and he began vomiting before the ship left the harbor. He took to his bed, a plastic trash can resting on his chest, Frances sitting on a chair nearby, Small Frank perched on her lap. In her hand was a drink that tasted, she said, like suntan lotion over ice.

She took advantage of Malcolm's captivity to catalog certain of her vast and multifaceted romantic excursions. "There was Raoul," she said. "The central casting Latin Lover. He used to always ask me, 'Will you remember this forever?' He was after immortality, I guess. He never did propose; he didn't want to *spend* forever with me. He only wanted me to recall him after he'd disappeared, which is what I'm doing now, of course— you're welcome, Raoul." She shrugged. "Then there was Kenneth, WASP wonder boy. We were involved in the premarriage courting ritual when he died in a car accident in Long Island. There's something about a person met with tragic death; you recall their living moments in a kinder light. We tell ourselves we knew on the psychic level they were going to die, but I didn't know, no. Joan was the one to tell me and it's true I cried but it felt forced and later I lay awake surprised at how little I cared. It's a shame he died that way, but I'm glad we never married. He wanted to tamp my spirit and he might have succeeded. But he was a beautiful boy—beautiful.

"Just on the heels of this came Charles, who was, unfortunately, Kenneth's married uncle. He cornered me at the wake; it was important that we speak, he told me. He took my wrist in his hand and I remember admiring his watch, a Rolex, and wondering at his hand's tan-ness. 'What are you doing in June?' he asked. He telephoned me the next morning with instructions to meet him on the first of the month at an airstrip outside New Jersey. 'Bring a passport, a swimsuit, and a good, long book,' he said. Being dutiful, I wrote these things down on a pad of paper. I taxied out and there was Charles, standing waiting beside the barb-wire fence walling in the tarmac. He wore short sleeves, sunglasses, and was smoking I swear to God a pipe. He took my bag and we walked toward the prop plane. 'How are you at keeping secrets?' he wanted to know. 'Fair,' I said. He thought I was being witty. When we returned, fourteen days later, I was more tan than he was, and he gave me his watch, along with a friendly chuck on the chin. He was thinking there'd be tears but my heart wasn't anywhere near broken. I'd read that good, long book twice through, and not because I found it worthy of revisiting. When the cabbie asked me where I'd been, I told him, 'Nowhere special,' and I gave him the Rolex as a tip. He thought it was a fake and I didn't bother to correct him. Everyone in Manhattan heard about the affair because I told them. Charles's marriage crumbled and he came around to chastise me, but also to ask if I'd run away with him. I said I wouldn't, and he vanished clear off the face of the earth. After this I became semi-infamous and was sought out by those hopeful for a suggestion of danger. My first sip of scandal. I can't claim to have disliked it. And it prepared me for what came later."

Malcolm sat up and retched into the trash can but nothing came. He settled back into his bed.

Frances said, "I ran from one brightly burning disaster to the next, pal. That's the way I was. Possibly you won't like to think of your mother as one who lived, but I'll tell you something: it's fun to run from one brightly burning disaster to the next."

Pointing to the cat, Malcolm said, "Tell me about him."

Frances stood and carried Small Frank to the door. She let him into the hall and returned, sitting and watching Malcolm with a patient expression.

"Tell me about your first date."

"The first date he took me to Tavern on the Green. He ate

his cupcake with a fork and knife, and I thought, *Who could love this man?*"

Malcolm said, "I can't imagine cupcakes at Tavern on the Green."

"That's a banal observation, Malcolm, but just to see the thought through, yes, they did for a time serve chocolate cupcakes at Tavern on the Green. He was nervous but hid it admirably. I liked that he wasn't afraid of silence." Frances became silent herself.

"Keep talking about him," said Malcolm.

"I don't want to."

"But did you love him?"

She was surprised by the question. She considered the answer. It seemed correct to respond honestly. "I did, then I didn't, then I did, then I *really* didn't."

A pause, and Malcolm began to vomit loudly into the trash can. Frances took this as her cue to retire. Some hours later, her telephone rang. Malcolm had found his sea legs, he said, and had scouted out the entire ship. "Did you know there's a medium on board? They've set her up in a little tent across from the buffet. Want to come visit her with me?"

Frances was unnerved by the idea of any sort of future-gazing, and said she wouldn't go; but she asked for a full report afterward, and Malcolm rang off, seeking out the medium abovedecks.

Approaching the tent, he thought he heard, then was sure he heard, the sound of someone in emotional distress. Peering into the moon-shaped window hole he saw two women, one young, one older. They sat facing each other before a low table crowded with candles and stone fruit and incense and tarot cards. The older woman was weeping; the young woman was not. "I'm sorry," said the latter. "I'm so sorry." The older woman seemed not to hear the words; soon she stood and rushed from the tent, fairly wailing, now. The young woman remained; she closed her eyes and rubbed her temples, speaking inaudibly to herself.

In studying her, Malcolm found her features favorable, and the atmosphere—the smoke, the dimness of the tent, the silky, soft-edged furnishing—felt intimate. She opened her eyes and, upon seeing Malcolm staring in at her, startled and shrieked. He hurried away, back down the stairs and to his room. Five minutes later a note shot under the door. Thinking it a rebuke from the medium, he was uneasy as he opened it. But it was only Frances writing with instructions for the evening.

# 9.

At the appointed time of eight P.M. Malcolm appeared in the dining hall wearing a tuxedo. He sat to the right of Frances, who was wearing a gown. In the chair to her left sat Small Frank, looking out the window at the black sky and blacker ocean. Frances also was staring; their heads were propped at the same degree of tilt. Malcolm asked her if she was all right and she answered, "I overheard a man say it was five miles to the bottom of the sea."

"Yes?" he said, sitting.

"Well, I wish I didn't know it. What a stupid thing to say on a cruise ship."

A waiter came to the table, a compactly handsome young man, thick black hair fixed in place. Pointing to Small Frank he asked, "Excuse me, whose cat is this?" When neither Malcolm nor Frances answered, he took Small Frank away. The cat hung limply in the waiter's hands and seemed bored by the fact of his removal. A moment passed when Frances suffered a guilt, or what passed for a guilt with her, and she went off to track the waiter down.

Malcolm fell to studying the dance floor, filled as it was with a game if aged crowd. They spun and jerked about to a surprisingly facile trio pumping out big-band tunes one on top of the other—which was strange when Malcolm considered that the seniors before him were twenty or thirty years too young to have taken part in the dance crazes they were now emulating with such relish. The older woman who'd been crying in the medium's tent had retrieved her cheer and was stepping through the crowd throwing fistfuls of confetti into the air. She looked perfectly enchanted to be doing this, as though it were all she'd ever wanted, to march about in a pink gown tossing confetti over the heads of strangers. The throng ate her up but Malcolm still could make out the occasional blast of confetti shot upward from the far side of the room. He was fishing a cherry from the bottom of Frances's drink when he saw the medium passing by. He hailed her; she approached and stood before him. "I'm Malcolm," he explained. When she didn't reply, he asked, "Will you tell me your name?"

"Madeleine."

"Madeleine, will you have a drink with me?"

"No."

"Just one drink, Madeleine?"

"No."

Frances returned, carrying Small Frank under her arm like a football. With the arrival of the cat, Madeleine's attitude completely changed. Dropping to a knee, she held his head in her hands and peered deeply into his eyes. Looking up at Frances, she said, "Interesting animal you've got here."

Frances asked Malcolm, "Who is this person?"

"Madeleine the medium."

"What's she doing?"

"I'm not sure. What are you doing, Madeleine?"

Madeleine stood. "Sorry." Pointing to Small Frank, she asked, "Do you not know?"

"We know," said Frances.

The handsome waiter returned. He was giving Madeleine a disapproving look; she in turn regarded him defiantly. She sat, pulling her chair close to Malcolm. "I think I will have that drink, actually." Addressing the waiter she said, "Dry gin martini."

"You know you're not supposed to sit here," the waiter told her.

"Don't be tedious, Salvatore."

"I'm not going to serve you."

Frances moved to stand before the waiter, Salvatore. "I'm sorry, good evening, hello," she said. "Is there some sort of problem?"

Salvatore blanched. "Good evening, ma'am. Yes, I'm afraid I can't serve the young lady in the dining area."

"And why is that?" she asked innocently.

"Since she works with us here, ma'am. It's company policy."

"A policy of segregation?"

"I don't know that segregation is the word."

"I think it is. Oh, but it's an ugly word, isn't it?"

"There's a very nice canteen for the ship's employees, ma'am."

Frances looked at Madeleine. Madeleine said, "It's dark and stinks of grease."

Frances studied Salvatore with her best unkind expression. "It was a dry gin martini, I believe," she said.

Salvatore was no match for Frances; he went away to fetch the drink. Madeleine said, "Hey, thanks," and Frances took up Small Frank's paw and made him salute. To Malcolm she said, "We're going to lie down."

"What about your dinner?"

"I'll order in. Will you come and see us later?"

Malcolm agreed, and Frances departed. After she'd gone Madeleine said, "She's neat. What's she paying you?"

"Paying me?"

"Aren't you her gigolo?"

"Oh my God," said Malcolm. "That's my mother."

Madeleine held up her hand. "Excuse me. But you'd be surprised at how common it is."

Salvatore soon returned to deliver Madeleine's drink. "You're a real fucking gentleman, Sally, you know that?" she said. She drank her first martini in under five minutes, then ordered and drank a second, then a third. The gin soothed her, and she became friendly, curious. When she asked after the specifics of Malcolm's life, he explained about Susan and his mother. "The town wasn't big enough for the two of them," he said.

"Which town is this?"

"New York City."

"But you're still engaged?"

"Technically. Does that bother you?"

"How could it?"

Malcolm asked her why the old woman in the tent had been crying and Madeleine said, "A quarter of the people on board this ship are in the presence of death. But if I say a single word about it? Off I go."

"You told the woman she's dying?"

"Yes, because she is."

"She seemed healthy enough last time I saw her." Here Malcolm explained about the woman's confetti performance on the dance floor. Madeleine listened with minimal interest. "She'll never see land again," she said.

Malcolm too was drinking, and the alcohol brought about a temporary mutual fondness, which led to an invitation to Madeleine's cabin, a cramped, airless space littered with dirty laundry and snack trash. The moment the door was shut behind them Madeleine pulled her gypsy dress over her head. She crawled into bed and Malcolm followed after. He knew the stimulation that accompanies unforeseen escapade; peeling off his socks, he said, "I won't be needing these!" Together, they experienced unremarkable intercourse. After, Madeleine's attitude soured. "I should be getting to sleep now," she said. Malcolm agreed, and laid his head on the pillow.

"I was asking you to leave," Madeleine told him.

Malcolm dressed and was reaching for the doorknob when there came a discreet tapping from the other side. He looked at Madeleine, but she had no reaction; she lay in her bunk looking vacantly upward. The knock reoccurred, louder, now. Malcolm felt certain it was a lover paying Madeleine a call: Salvatore? It was three o'clock in the morning and Malcolm's flesh was burning with fatigue. He knew he couldn't face whoever stood in the hall, but neither could he return to lie beside Madeleine. He closed his eyes standing up, feeling the slow sway of water beneath his feet. Five miles—what a terrible fact of nature it was. He thought of the subsumed ship gliding nose-first all that way in darkness, and of the eventual slow-motion collision with the sandy ocean floor.

# 10.

Frances was in her bed, in her indigo robe, hair upswept, studying herself in a palm mirror and talking to Small Frank, who was sitting beside her and listening with what could be interpreted as interest. "It's like a retirement, in a way," she explained. "Though, no, I've never worked, and so what mantle is being retired, even. And then, who retires *after* the money's all gone." She made a face describing a shrug. She lowered her mirror and looked at Small Frank. "I'm not sure how we're going to get you into Europe," she said. She raised her mirror and sucked in her cheeks. "All that lovely money." She observed a moment of silence before turning the bedside light off.

## 11.

Days passed. Nothing happened. The ocean was larger than Frances had imagined, and she wished the ship would go faster. On the last night of the cruise she and Malcolm were invited to dine at the captain's table. The captain was in his middle sixties, traditionally handsome, full head of silver hair. He ordered his steak bloody and drank Scotch on ice and was enamored of Frances from the moment he saw her; quip after quip passed his lips for her benefit but she offered him not even fleeting eye contact. She wasn't ignoring him intentionally, it was only that she was lost in a meandering mental phase and hadn't registered his existence. When a dish broke in the kitchen, she stirred and surveyed the table. The captain was watching her expectantly. "I'm moving to Paris," she told him.

"Yes, that was my understanding. Are you very excited?"

"I suppose I should be."

"I admire you for carving out a second act for yourself." He raised a glass in her direction. "Bravo."

"Thank you," said Frances. "But it's the third act if we're to be honest. Or the coda, if you'd rather."

The captain appeared troubled. He leaned over and whispered in the ear of the young man sitting next to him. This person was the captain's underling, and the resemblance was such they could have been related. The underling listened intently, and once the comment or instruction was completed he left the table. The captain resumed his conversation with Frances:

"And your son is coming along with you, isn't that right?"

"Of course," she said. She patted Malcolm's hand, and he looked generally in her direction but said nothing. He was thinking of Madeleine the medium. He hadn't seen her since their dalliance; the day before he'd sought her out in her tent, but an off-duty sign hung over the entrance. And he'd knocked on her cabin door before dinner—no answer. Salvatore was working the far side of the dining hall and Malcolm waved to him but he didn't wave back.

"I find it refreshing to see a child so devoted," the captain continued. "It's all I can do to get my daughter to speak with me on the phone." Quietly, as though it were half a secret, he said, "I was close with my mother, too."

"I despised mine," said Frances.

"Did you?"

"Despised."

Aiming for tact, the captain said, "The burden of motherhood can be a strain."

"She was a demon. And if such a place as hell exists then

that's where she collects her mail." Frances signaled the waiter for another drink.

The captain was unsure how to respond, and so sat in silence, watching his steak and wondering if Frances was crazy, and furthermore if that made a difference. Frances's drink was delivered and she took a sip. Recalling the daunting fact she had learned the day before, she asked, "Is it true that it's five miles to the bottom of the sea?"

The captain could hardly think of something he would rather have been asked, and he all but leapt up to answer. "At its deepest it's still shy of that, but just. We're talking about the Mariana Trench, here. That's in the western Pacific—far enough away that it might not exist so far as we're concerned. Five miles is an uncommon depth, however. Where we are now, it's more along the line of two miles."

The news was a balm for Frances, and the aggregate gin was having its effect. To her own surprise she suddenly found the captain physically attractive. He was a buffoon and she knew it but what was there to lose, at this late date, in straightforward fun? The captain deduced she thought him winning and lit up, inhabiting his most rakish persona. They leaned in close to each other, their voices husky and low.

"Have you many compatriot seamen?" Frances asked.

"A good number."

"Have any been swallowed up by the Deep?"

"I'm sorry to say it but yes."

"And do you ever awake in fright for fear of following after them?"

"I have, Frances, and I have." The captain's underling came back and passed him a folded slip of paper before returning to his seat and staring dead ahead with a mysterious vigilance. The captain discreetly opened and read the note, nodded, and tucked it away in his coat pocket. The underling still was staring; Frances asked the captain, "Is this young man a relative of yours?"

"No."

"He could be your son by the looks of him."

"Yes, that's true, but no, he's not."

"What's his name?"

"Douglas, but I like to call him Dugger."

"Isn't that nice?" She leaned over. "May I call you Dugger also?"

"Yes, ma'am," answered Dugger. He blushed a flaming pink, and Frances was moved by the young man's shyness and fine manners. "Out of the blue, and I feel so happy!" she said. The captain sensed his moment had arrived and laid a hand atop Frances's. She looked at it, and he looked at her looking at it, then he himself looked at it. Malcolm also was looking at it; now he looked away, and at the older gentleman sitting on his left. The man wore a poorly fitted, well-worn white linen suit and he was sweating heavily, his breathing labored, his face the color of rare beef. He was staring at a glass of tequila fitted into his hand. Malcolm nudged him and the man flinched, inhaling sharply through his nostrils. "What?" he asked, not looking away from his drink.

"I'm Malcolm Price."

"Good for you. I'm Boris Maurus."

"Your name is Boris Maurus?"

"Yeah."

Malcolm considered this. He said, "We both have horror-movie names."

The man turned to face Malcolm. "May be," he said. "But I

wouldn't know because I don't watch horror movies, because my life is already a horror movie, so what's the point?"

"Okay," said Malcolm.

"I watch documentaries."

"All right."

This man was the ship's doctor. When Malcolm inquired after his mood, the doctor acknowledged that the voyage had been a difficult one. "Some moron posing as a gypsy told one of the passengers she was dying, which is bad enough, but then the woman really did die."

"Do you mean Madeleine?"

"The gypsy? I think that's her name. You know her?"

Malcolm said he did, and mentioned Madeleine's disappearance. The doctor, nodding, said, "Oh, they threw her in the jug."

"The jug?"

"The brig."

"Can they do that?"

"You're goddamned right they can." The doctor drank half his tequila. "A middling lawyer could prove your buddy murdered that woman. Threat of violence leading to cardiac arrest." He snapped his fingers. "These old birds spook if you say boo at them. Once Death's on deck? In a contained environment? They freak fucking out. I've seen it. It's grim."

"What are they going to do with her?"

"Your buddy? Probably they'll kick her off the ship at Calais. Or else they'll keep her in the jug until the ship returns to the States. One way or the other, she's out on her ass." He finished his tequila, Malcolm his whiskey. A waiter stood nearby and they both waved and pointed at their empty glasses but the man walked away.

"Do you have many emergencies at sea?" Malcolm asked.

The doctor made a sour face. "You have no idea." He leaned in, a bent light in his eye. "Insider secret," he whispered. "A cruise ship is a death ship."

The waiter returned, and again Malcolm and the doctor waved to him, and again he didn't see them or was pretending not to see them. Before he could get away, Boris Maurus lunged, grabbing the waiter by his sleeve.

"Excuse me," said the waiter.

"I will not excuse you until you recognize our desire."

"Please let go, sir."

"Will you recognize it, yes or no?"

The waiter soon brought them their drinks. The doctor took a long sip and gasped. "I could show you something very terrible, if you'd like," he said.

"Yes," said Malcolm.

They went away from the dining hall, descending a series of increasingly narrow stairwells, where the air grew stale. Together they entered a servants' elevator, small enough that the men's stomachs were touching. The ice in their drinks was chiming lightly as they arrived at the medical office. The doctor asked Malcolm to wait for him, then left by a metal door, on the face of which was a handmade sign that read: CHILL ZONE. The words were illustrated in such a way as to appear fabricated of solid ice. Malcolm lay his palm on the door and it was, indeed, quite cold.

He sat at the doctor's desk, flipping through the man's workbook. At the start there were patient names, symptoms, medicines administered, etc.; then came a series of drawings: a clutch of pansies, an empty rowboat, a study of hands in various gripping and reaching positions. These renderings were neither good nor bad; they represented someone with a passing interest in figurative drawing and a degree of ability but no great verve or passion for it. There was one drawing that made an impression on Malcolm, however. It was of a most houselike house, with the requisite four-way windowpanes, picket fencing, tidy garden, shingled roof—all the familiar attributes of the idealized American home. Issuing from the brick chimney, sketched in a wispy font and bobbing along on the air, were the words: *Death, a smoke—it enters the nostrils and exits the mouth!*

The words made Malcolm unaccountably uncomfortable. He closed the notebook and stood away from the table, unsure what to do next. He hadn't precise control of his limbs and admitted to himself, "I've had too much to drink." Now the doctor returned, smiling and holding a full shot glass in each hand. "Try this," he said.

"What is it?"

The doctor passed one to Malcolm. "Palinka. Hungarian brandy."

Malcolm sniffed the liquid and recoiled. "I don't want to drink this."

"You have to."

"Why?"

"Because it's fun. You and me. Drinking drinks." He raised his glass to cheers Malcolm; Malcolm drank half the brandy in a bolt. The heat of it made him retch. "Strong," he said wheezily, and shivered. "It's quite strong."

"It'll kill you," said the doctor, and drank his palinka down. He beckoned for Malcolm to follow him into the CHILL ZONE; Malcolm was plunged into refrigerated cold as he entered the ship's morgue. He found himself standing over the corpse of the old woman he'd seen dancing and tossing confetti. She lay on a slab the doctor had pulled from the wall. She was still in her pink gown, confetti in her hair, but her face was ghoulish and gray and all the life, the loveliness, had gone out of her.

Malcolm was sometimes frustrated by his own inability to experience emotion, but in this moment it seemed he was feeling too much. It was not sadness or revulsion but something more like a too-loud noise in his ears. Behind him, the doctor was pulling out the other slabs, each of these holding a corpse, nine in total. Malcolm cast about in his mind for the meaning of this spectacle.

The room had been empty, and now it was full.

"What happened to them?" Malcolm asked.

"Just that they died," replied the doctor.

"We haven't been at sea a week."

"You get a body a day. That's the industry standard for an Atlantic crossing. I've a theory that they come to sea because subconsciously they know they're dying. Some ancient Nordic impulse, maybe." Boris Maurus was smiling; Malcolm wanted to get away from him. He finished his palinka and set the glass on the slab before him. The doctor stared at it. "What's the matter?" he asked.

"I think what it is is that I'm feeling sleepy."

A heaviness came over the doctor. It seemed Malcolm had disappointed him in some significant yet familiar way. "Thanks for showing me this," Malcolm said, edging toward the exit. The doctor only shrugged. "I won't tell anyone about it."

"Tell whoever you want."

Malcolm left the CHILL ZONE. He felt queasy, and craved fresh air, but when he went abovedecks the wind nearly bowled him over the railing. Returning to the ship's interior, he wandered awhile. He realized he'd misplaced his key, and he couldn't remember his or Frances's room number, or even their floor— and he couldn't think of what to do in answer to this. At last he became so tired he sought out a dark corner, sat down, and slept. Some hours later he awoke, startled by a pink light creeping over his legs: the dawn. He'd fallen asleep cross-legged and couldn't move his legs for a time, but had to stretch out and wait for the circulating blood to rejuvenate them.

# 12.

After Malcolm and the doctor had gone off together, Frances and the captain also continued drinking; and when the captain asked Frances to visit his quarters she agreed, following him down long corridors. He had unhooked his clip-on tie; he held a bottle of champagne by its throat and was whistling "Hershey Bar." His room was orderly, faceless. *I'm going to fuck the captain,* Frances thought. But he was a man past his prime, and very little was accomplished in his room that night. Frances was impressed by how unbothered he was by his impotency. "It's very common," he said.

"I've never experienced it," Frances admitted.

"Very, very common." Altogether it was as alarming to him as a Wet Paint sign on a park bench, it seemed. "Who's got room for more?" he asked, popping the bottle and pouring out two glasses. It was low-quality champagne but the bubbles fizzed pleasantly against Frances's lips and she was amused at her evening's detour. It occurred to her that, so long as she maintained forward motion, her life could not not continue, a comforting equation that conjured in her a sense of empowerment and ease. She and the captain were lying together in naked embrace, the both of them staring down at the captain's penis, a glum mushroom caving in on itself.

"Tell me a bedtime story," the captain said.

"I don't think I know any bedtime stories," Frances answered. She thought awhile. "I could tell you about Olivia."

"Perfect," said the captain, and he closed his eyes.

"Olivia," said Frances, "was my governess. She called me Miss Walnut, but I can't remember why. She had a half-hidden limp, her homeliness summoned double takes, and her private life was, so far as I could tell, joyless. She'd been my governess since I could walk and was more a mother to me than my own ever was. I loved her very much, do you understand? And she loved me, also. We were close for many years, but as I grew older, then our relationship started to change.

"By the age of eleven I was becoming beautiful, so that people began acting strangely because of it. Certain women were cruel to me, for example. They were unshy about this—they wanted me to appreciate their dislike of me. Men, of course, were deferential in a way I'd still call sexual. There weren't any advances; I wasn't molested. They were simply looking to the future, putting a pin in something that might be addressed later. Besides all this, I was discovering about money. What it meant to have as much as we had then, I mean, and how rare it was not to have to worry. In short, I was learning that my life was wide open. This went to my head, and I began to affect the airs of my elders:

making cutting remarks about people after they'd left the room, sending back food in restaurants, things like that."

The captain's eyes still were closed but he wasn't yet sleeping.

Frances said, "As the snobby phase took hold, Olivia pulled away from me. There was a period of gentle chastisement, I remember. This was followed by a peevishness. Then came a general avoidance. One night I was getting into a bath she'd prepared for me. The water was too hot, so that it burned my foot, and without thinking I spun around and snapped at her. What was she trying to do, cook me? She stared for a while, then began moving toward me. She had such an odd look in her eye; I think she was afraid of her own anger." She poked the captain in the ribs. "Do you know what she did next? Do you want to guess?"

The captain opened his eyes but said nothing.

"She drew back her hand, and she slapped me so hard in the face that my head almost came off from my shoulders!"

"Yes," said the captain. He closed his eyes again. "Then what?"

"She went away and I got into the bath and sat in the hot water. My cheek was tingling, and I couldn't stop shaking. I put myself to bed that night and in the morning Olivia was friendly, as though we'd had some small disagreement. After a week, or a month, she said, 'Miss Walnut, have you forgotten what happened in the bath?'

"'No,' I said.

"'But why haven't you told anyone about it?'

"'I don't know. I just don't want to.'" Frances sipped the champagne. The captain's head was dipped; he was sleeping, now. Frances stared at him for a long while. She drew a lock of silver hair away from his simple face. "I never did tell on her," she said. "It was something just for us to share. And I knew it was important, even then. Such complicated information, delivered with such concision."

Frances dressed. The doctor had hung his coat on the back of a chair and she noticed the slip of paper peeking from the breast pocket. It was a handwritten note: *Coda: the concluding passage of a piece or movement, typically forming an addition to the basic structure.* And after that: *Hope this helps, Cap! Dugger.*

Frances, smiling, folded the note and returned it to the captain's pocket. She had occasionally in her life found herself loving men not in spite of but for their stupidity. Suavity was never more than playacting, she knew this, and it endeared them to her that they themselves were unaware of their transparency. She hung her shoes from her hooked fingers, walking barefoot along the dim, carpeted halls to her suite. All were asleep and it was so quiet, and she felt very youthful and glad. Small Frank was up, waiting on the bed. His eyes narrowed as she entered. "Spare me," she said. "You haven't got a leg to stand on." She moved to the bathroom to draw herself a bath. Now she was whistling "Hershey Bar."

# 13.

Malcolm and Frances met in the morning and discussed their respective oceanic exploits. Regarding the doctor and his cadavers, Frances had little to say; she was more interested in Malcolm's relationship with Madeleine the medium.

"You made love to her?"

"Well, yes."

"Did you do a good job?"

"Not a very good one, no."

"Do you normally do a good job?"

"Sometimes I do. I think the problem is that I don't care enough."

Frances said, "If you do one thing well, it might as well be that."

Malcolm pondered this. He asked if the captain had done a good job and Frances said, "Don't be tacky, pal." Small Frank sulked in the background; Frances whispered to Malcolm, "How are we meant to get him into France?" Since their embarkation, she'd felt increasingly anxious that they were three together, not two, and that if Small Frank were left behind, then some piece of their luck would also fall away. She decided she would drug and smuggle him across the border in her purse, a seemingly simple scheme that in actuality posed disastrous potential. She had a bottleful of Valium, but how does one give Valium to a cat? And how much should be given that Small Frank would doze but not expire? After some consideration, and with the boat an hour from the port at Calais, she ground up five five-milligram pills into a portion of tuna salad and set this out for him before taking in the air abovedecks one final time. When she returned, she found him splayed on the bathroom floor and rolled him into her bag amid stacks of cash. She endeavored to think of the operation as chic in the cloak-and-dagger style, but Small Frank was snoring, the heft of the bag tantamount to manual labor, and she soon succumbed to self-pity. To combat this, and finding herself envious of the cat's state, she also took five Valium.

It was a hazy day, and the rank air at Calais clung to the flesh. They entered the line for customs; ahead of them was Madeleine the medium. She was ducking down to avoid being seen by Malcolm, which he noticed but chose to ignore. He pushed ahead of the crowd, tapping her on the shoulder. She gave a half turn. "Hello," she said.

"Here's our jailbird now."

"Here I am."

"And you've paid your debt to society?"

"Yes, very funny." She was wan and chalky and Malcolm asked if she was sick. "No, just mortified," she said.

Malcolm nodded. Looking around, he sniffed and said, "Smells different here."

Madeleine sniffed and shrugged.

"It's invigorating," Malcolm added.

Now Frances approached, on shaky legs, clutching at people as she passed them by. "Oh, your little witchy friend," she said. "How do you do?"

"Hello," said Madeleine. "I hope you haven't lost that cat?"

Frances opened the purse and Madeleine peered in. "He's having his siesta until we're through customs."

Madeleine asked, "Is that real money?"

"Of course. I don't think that there's anything so comforting as quite a lot of money, don't you agree with me?"

"I wouldn't know."

"Try it sometime and tell me if it isn't just the thing to chase your blues away."

It registered with Malcolm that something was amiss with Frances. She was mumbling to herself; she was repressing laughter; twice she stepped on his toes. "Are you drunk?" he whispered. "Noooooo," she replied. Before he could uncover what was the matter with her, they had arrived at the front of the line. Madeleine went before them and passed through; the customs agent motioned for Malcolm and Frances to come forward. He asked what the purpose of their trip was and Frances, leaning an elbow on the countertop, said, "Chasing after youthful fantasies," then winked.

"Madame?"

"We're vacationists. I want to see the Eiffel Tower, then die."

"Die?" The customs agent shook his head. "But you are not so old, madame."

She said, "I'm old enough to have received a corsage from a white-gloved West Point cadet with a pomaded ducktail and a solid silver flask of rye in the pocket of his gabardine tuxedo—*that's* how old I am."

The customs agent was flummoxed. He asked Malcolm, "She is sick, monsieur?"

"She isn't sick."

"She does not die?"

"Never."

"She must not die here," the customs agent warned Malcolm.

"She'll die somewhere else," Malcolm promised.

The customs agent looked back at Frances. "No dying in France." He stamped their passports and waved them on. They purchased train tickets, Frances digging out the cash beneath Small Frank, who was yet inert. They settled into the first-class compartment and Frances slept while Malcolm read the account of the voyages of Christopher Columbus: *7 September. All Friday he was becalmed.*

Madeleine approached and sat opposite him. She was eating a sandwich from the bar car, a blank look on her face. It seemed to Malcolm she wasn't going to say a word, then she ticktocked her head, swallowed, and told him, "I couldn't send her back to the conga line without telling her."

"Maybe people don't want to know."

"Of course they want to know. Wouldn't you want to?"

"No."

"Well, I told her, and I don't feel bad about it."

Malcolm asked, "How did you know to tell her?"

"I've been able to see it coming since I was a little girl."

"But how?"

"Toward the end, there's a color."

"What color?"

"Green."

A ticket taker arrived and stood before them. Malcolm handed over his and his mother's ticket and the man punched them, then asked in French for Madeleine's.

"What's he saying?" she asked.

"He wants your ticket," Malcolm told her.

"I haven't got one."

"*Madame n'a pas de billet, monsieur,*" said Malcolm.

The ticket taker asked Malcolm if the young lady wished to purchase a first- or second-class ticket; if it was the latter, he said, she would have to relocate to another compartment. Malcolm interpreted for Madeleine, who said, "I don't want to buy either. He can kick me off the train if he wants to but I've got five hundred dollars to my name and I'm going to need it in Paris."

The ticket taker had his credit card reader at the ready and wore an expectant, happy expression. When Malcolm explained what Madeleine had told him, the card reader slowly dropped, and the ticket taker looked hurt. The young woman was putting him in a bad place, he said. Malcolm expressed sympathy but said that she herself was in a bad place, and that that sort of thing had a tendency to spread. The ticket taker did not disagree with this, but said he resented Madeleine for upsetting what he called the graceful balance of his work. He would not kick her off the train but said he believed she could represent herself better if she strove to do so. He moved away, down the aisle.

"What did he say?" asked Madeleine.

"He's unimpressed with you, but he's not going to kick you off the train."

Madeleine finished her sandwich, balled up the trash, and dropped it on the ground at her feet. Standing, she pointed at Frances's purse. "You could have just bought me a ticket, you know." Malcolm told her the truth, which was that the thought hadn't occurred to him. Madeleine turned to leave.

"Where are you going?"

"I really don't know, Malcolm," she said, and then she was gone.

Frances awoke minutes before the train landed at Gare du Nord. She smiled sleepily. "I never wanted to live one life," she said. "I wanted to live three lives." Small Frank rustled in her purse. It was nighttime in Paris, mid-December, the city made up with Christmas accents, bodies surging in all directions.

# PARIS

## 14.

Joan's apartment was located at the easternmost tip of the Île Saint-Louis. It was on the fifth floor and consisted of two bedrooms connected by a long, slender hallway; at the midpoint between the rooms were a modest kitchen, bathroom, and living room. As a habitable space it was serviceable, but without any trace of grandiosity, and with their own previously owned and comparably lavish apartment only a short walk away, Frances felt desolate at the sight of it. "It puts the *apart* in apartment," said Malcolm, but his mother could not be cheered. Neither she nor Malcolm could sleep that night, and both were up before sunrise. There was nothing to eat, no coffee or tea; they dressed and struck out with no destination in mind.

The fact of their being in Paris was different than it had been with past visits; now they were there because it was required, and this was somehow meant to be their home. They were lonely in their silence but neither could summon a topic of conversation. Shopkeepers were raising their shutters and hosing off the sidewalks; Frances was cold, and suggested they visit a church. Thinking of the view on this bright winter day, Malcolm said they should go to Sacré-Cœur.

"Sacré-Cœur is a casino," said Frances.

"Notre-Dame?"

"To stand in line with the morons?"

"Saint-Sulpice?"

"Oh, well, fine."

Actually, Frances preferred Saint-Sulpice to all other churches in Paris; this was the church she'd had in mind when she brought it up. But she was embarrassed to like something so patently likable. It was good of Malcolm to play along, she thought. They crossed the Île Saint-Louis and walked up the Boulevard Saint-Germain. The city was awakening, traffic thickening; crossing the street, Frances took Malcolm's hand in hers.

Saint-Sulpice was dark and grand, the air thick and warm. In response to a nameless cue they parted at the entrance, Malcolm following a counterclockwise line, Frances clockwise. She stopped to admire each of the chapels, dropping a bill into the box marked *Chapelle des Ames-du-Purgatoire*. She lit a candle and set it upright on the altar, gazing at the flame and thinking of her curious relationship with the Church.

Growing up she had had no religion; in fact the first time she'd set foot in a church was for her mother's funeral. She was fifteen years old, and had felt powerful standing over the corpse of her tormentor. Looking up at Christ's admirable rib cage, she quietly told him, "I'm glad she's dead. Thank you for killing her." She didn't expect an answer, and she had no need for dialogue, but after she left the church she felt unburdened. Over the years she'd found it beneficial to visit churches from time to time and share her darker thoughts.

At Franklin's funeral she felt impenetrable, which isn't to say strong, but resilient, nonporous—a leaden rod. Being expressly barred, she'd snuck in with the crowd, face covered by a veil. Standing beside the coffin—closed, naturally—she pulled the veil back, and all in the church turned to watch, to wonder and gape at her gall. Out of the crowd came Carlson Wallace, Franklin's second in command at the firm; he approached Frances with his hands outstretched, not to greet her but to remove her, bodily if need be. He took her by the arm and led her to the exit. He deposited her on the steps of the church and returned to the funeral. He had looked at Frances as though she were a fiend capable of violence. A lurching pipe organ accompanied her departure. She placed her veil in a trash can and followed after the thin warmth of an autumn sun, away and into the park.

The pews at Saint-Sulpice consisted of oak and wicker chairs connected at the leg by long rods. Frances sat; her chair creaked and snapped dryly, loudly. She removed her gloves and folded her hands in her lap. Speaking lowly, and generally upward, she gave voice to her private, two-part plan. It was a relief to say the words, but also frightening, for the plan became suddenly concrete, and there was the sense of a countdown's commencement. Her hands were trembling; she waited for this to pass before standing to seek out Malcolm.

She found him sitting on the far side of the church, looking at nothing and thinking of it. Malcolm had less of a reason for visiting a church than his mother. He didn't take the notion of God seriously but couldn't deny the feeling of beatitude he knew when he sat in a church pew. He attributed this to aesthetics; he wasn't conflicted about it.

"Are you up for a spree?" Frances asked. Part one of the two-part plan was to spend every penny they had.

"I don't need anything."

"You need an overcoat and I need a dress."

Recalling the heft of her luggage, Malcolm asked, "What do you need a dress for?"

"An uncommon engagement. Are you up for a spree or aren't you?"

Together they left Saint-Sulpice, taxiing to the Galeries Lafayette. Shopping for Frances was a healthful exercise, and she went about it with determination and diligence. Malcolm did not dislike it but possessed such a meager vanity that clothing held only a minimal appeal. Frances forced him to try on several coats and bought him a houndstooth Burberry trench. For herself she purchased a deep-red, raw-silk Chanel cocktail dress. Malcolm wore the coat out; Frances rolled her dress like a cigarette and tucked it into her purse.

They stood on the sidewalk in front of the Galeries Lafayette breathing exhaust and watching the tide of humanity wash past. Travel fatigue was setting in and Frances wished to return to the apartment but Malcolm suggested they stay awake until nightfall, that they might correct their clocks. Neither of them was hungry but they entered a nondescript bistro for an early dinner. The waiter disliked Malcolm and Frances from the moment he saw them, and made no attempt to hide this, refusing to address them in French and seating them next to the men's toilet. Malcolm and Frances found it amusing for a time—here was the legendary rude French waiter made flesh—but it was half an hour before the wine arrived, and an evil smell came from under the men's room door, and with their fatigue becoming more acute, the situation grew tiresome. Without speaking of it they both had the sense of being tested by the Fates, and both decided they could and would rally and endure the occasion. The wine was off and they drank it and ordered a second bottle. The food was cold and it was awful and they ate it.

Now came the trial of paying the bill. The waiter was annoyed by their refusal to take noticeable offense at his discourtesies, and decided he would make them wait longer than any other customers had waited before. Malcolm waved three separate times but the waiter, standing idly at the bar, merely waved back. Malcolm crossed the restaurant and asked for the bill directly; the waiter nodded and said, "Soon, buddy," then went outside and made a show of smoking not one but two cigarettes, exhaling as he watched them watching him.

Frances had had enough. She pulled a bottle of perfume from her bag and began spritzing the bouquet of flowers in the center of the table. The waiter looked on from the sidewalk, wondering what she was playing at. Malcolm knew, and he studied his mother admiringly as she removed her lighter from her coat pocket: *click!* She held the flame to the bouquet and it went up in a ball. The restaurant had filled up by this point, and nearby customers stood away from their tables, cutlery clanking to the floor, the light of the fire dancing in their frightened eyes. The waiter rushed over to stand before the blaze in speechless disbelief. "*L'addition, s'il vous plaît,*" Frances told him. Malcolm sat beaming. The waiter ran off in search of a fire extinguisher.

# 15.

A week after their arrival, Frances entered Malcolm's room and set twenty thousand euros on his pillow. "For walking around," she said.

A piece of mail had arrived, an invitation to a dinner party scheduled for that same evening. The inviter was unknown to them, one Mme Reynard; at the bottom of the card were the words, *Please come!! You will find yourself among friends!!!*

"What do you think of that?" Frances asked Malcolm.

"Too many exclamation points."

"But do you think we should go?"

"Late notice. But sure, I'm up for it if you are."

Frances spent the afternoon getting ready. She had in her youth thought of her beauty as something to be weaponized, something capable of inflicting pain, and now this feeling returned to her. A good many of her invitations in New York during the previous decades had been rooted in a certain macabre social value she possessed as the grisly widow of Franklin Price; she had the sense this was the reason for her invitation now, and she wanted to arrive looking so attractive as to smite whoever opened the door. Hatred was a fillip and she was glad in her preparations.

The party was located near the Place des Vosges and they set out on foot in the early evening with Small Frank leading the way. It occurred to Malcolm that his mother and father had been to Paris without him, and he asked her about this. "I've been coming since I was a young girl, of course." She pointed at the cat. "But he'd never been until I insisted. Actually, we spent our honeymoon here."

"I can't picture the two of you on a honeymoon."

Frances shrugged. "It was all the normal things. Hotels and flowers and champagne. It's strange to think he was actually fun, but in the beginning he really was. We went to the Luxembourg Garden and I noticed him watching the children beside the pond with their sailboats and long sticks. I rented one for him and he set about following the boat with his stick, a glad, stupid look on his face. We were twenty-five years old. He lost interest in the boat and it floated away; then we started feeding the carp bits of a hot dog I was eating. They went berserk for it, and there was something about all these grotesquely fat fish piling on top of one another, and for a *hot dog*—it made me laugh, hard. I never laugh like that anymore, and rarely did then. I think your father was surprised by it. Well, he went away and came back with six hot dogs." She looked at Malcolm. "He'd bought them because he wanted to make me laugh again. Do you understand?"

"Yes."

"Such a small gesture," she said, "but it couldn't have been further away from the man I knew later. A groundskeeper came over and asked us to please *refrain* from feeding hot dogs to the carp. Your father's response was to toss the hot dogs and stick into the pond. The groundskeeper and sailboat rental man both were shouting after us as we left the garden, but it was like we couldn't hear them. Our arms were linked. We were making plans for dinner, I remember."

The story made Malcolm feel solemn. Frances squinted at her son. "What do *you* remember about him?"

Malcolm didn't remember much, but two moments stood out. The first was a trip to the Central Park Zoo when he was eight. It had been going well enough at the start; they weren't sharing anything significant but it was something, time together, a modest experience, but real. They drifted from cage to cage, saying nothing. Malcolm had wanted to know his father so badly in those days, and he wondered if this wasn't the beginning of an understanding between them. Then came the gorillas.

When they entered the monkey house, the gorillas were lazing about peaceably, docile in their fabricated jungle. But the moment Franklin took up his position at the glass they stirred, became agitated. Soon they were howling and circling the cage, every one of them taken up with a collective outrage. Franklin had watched the shift in the gorillas' mood with an amused bafflement, but as it became clearer he was the focus of their hostility, his expression grew more severe. Now the largest gorilla approached and stood before him, shrieking and pounding at the glass. Reaching down, he shat in his hand and smeared his waste at the level of Franklin's face. Franklin yanked Malcolm away by his wrist, dragging him to the ticket booth to formally protest. The woman in the booth was afraid of Franklin; his anger was acute and his complaint sounded like paranoiac raving. "You're saying the gorillas didn't like you, sir?" She assured him it wasn't personal, but that was just it: it was. Franklin had been singled out by distant relatives as one unfit to live among them, and he felt the sting of tribal ostracism. He got his money back, a bitter victory. Malcolm sensed his father blamed the incident on him. Years passed before he would be alone with him again.

Malcolm's second memory told of the time his father had brought him along to a father/son function at the Metropolitan Club. The other children seemed far more competent than Malcolm was—miniature men who understood the value of wit, who knew that socializing was a game of consequence. They had their schools and professions selected, and their fathers were proud, affectionate, present, whereas his own father had gone off to some secret chamber and left him to sit and chat with a sleepy bartender named Sam. Malcolm drank four cherry colas in a row and vomited on the carpet of the foyer. His father was called for; when he saw the vomit, he pressed a hundred dollars into Sam's hand. "Clean him up and put him in a cab. He knows the address." Franklin left the room, cigar smoke cresting over his shoulder. Sam looked at the hundred-dollar bill, then Malcolm, who wore a bib of cooling bile that was seeping into the top of his boxer shorts. "All right, kid," he said.

Malcolm told these stories to Frances but she wasn't listening very closely. She was studying the party invitation. Pointing at the building before them, she said, "This is us." Small Frank was no longer with them, having chased after a plump, hobbling gutter mouse.

# 16.

A bell rung, a door opened: Mme Reynard. Frances had prepared herself to face off against a roomful of impeccably dressed French women of high social standing. It was to be a night of implied insults and needling insinuations and she could hardly wait to get started. But the woman standing before them wore slacks and a baggy sweater, and she smiled and spoke English in an American accent. "Oh, hey, you made it!" She ushered them in, took their coats, and led them through the apartment to the dining room. The table was set for three; Frances experienced a lesser horror.

"We're not early?" she said.

"No, right on time."

"Where are the others?"

"There are no others but us," said Mme Reynard. "Would either of you like a martini? I've been waiting all day for mine."

"I would like a martini," said Malcolm.

"Frances?" said Mme Reynard.

Frances nodded, and Mme Reynard left to prepare the drinks. Frances turned to Malcolm. "What the fuck is going on here?" she asked, and Malcolm shrugged. He sat and waited for his drink while Frances moved around the dining room to assess the furnishings and artworks, hopeful these would be lacking in some way. Mme Reynard had passable taste, however, and Frances, seeing no exploitable weakness, sat beside Malcolm at the dinner table. Mme Reynard returned with the martinis on a tray. The three of them drank and Malcolm and Mme Reynard made approving noises but Frances only stared. When Mme Reynard said, "I'm so happy you came," Frances didn't respond. The silence felt hostile; Mme Reynard thought to combat it with biographical information. "I married a Frenchman in my twenties," she explained. "There was nothing keeping me in the States, so when he wanted to return to Paris, I went along with it. He died this summer, and afterward I realized our friends were actually his friends, and that not only did I not like them, but they didn't like me, either. Haven't seen a single one of them since the funeral. I don't miss them particularly, but I miss the noise they made. That's why I invited you over, because I'm lonely."

Frances felt burdened, even revolted by the admission. "How'd your husband die?" she asked.

"He choked to death."

"That's a new one."

"It was a very ugly thing."

Frances scoffed and sipped her martini. Mme Reynard was watching her. "Please don't be cruel to me," she said. "It was difficult to get up the nerve to invite you over."

Frances said, "I suppose I don't see why we're here, is all."

"Just that I was curious to meet you. Of course, I know who you are. I grew up in New York City, and we're the same age, about. We all thought you were so wonderful, my friends and I."

"I see."

"So wonderful. And so, I hoped we could become friends."

"I appreciate that. But the fact is that I have no need of friends in my life at the moment."

"Everyone needs friends," Mme Reynard said.

"No, that's actually not true."

"Well," said Mme Reynard. "I'm sorry to hear that that's the way you feel. But you're here now, and I've made a cassoulet, and I vote we make the best of it. What do you think? Malcolm? Shall we make the best of it?"

Malcolm said, "Yes."

"Fine," said Mme Reynard. "Will you have another martini before the wine?"

"Yes, please," said Malcolm.

Mme Reynard went away again. Malcolm told Frances, "You're being a dick."

"Isn't it awful?" Frances gripped her hands into fists. "I'm sorry. I'll stop."

When Mme Reynard came back, Frances thanked her for the drink. She was sitting upright, her features were softer, and she became inquisitive.

"So, Mme Reynard, what do you do every day?"

"Oh, what a terrible question," Mme Reynard said. "Since my husband died I've become something of the tourist. Museums, opera, ballet."

"Didn't he like to do those types of things?"

"No, and neither did I, and neither do I, but I don't know how else to pass the time." She pointed at Frances. "Do you know, he died in that very chair."

Frances suddenly became aware of the chair's dimensions. It was an exciting thing to know and she was happy she'd been told about it.

"What did he choke *on?*" she asked.

"Ah, lamb."

"And have you eaten lamb since?"

"No. But, you know, I never liked lamb much in the first place."

"I don't either. The gamy meats somehow summon the fact of the animal's existence, which puts me in mind of its death."

"I've never thought of it before."

"Whereas a steak is simply a steak."

"Yes, that's right."

"May I ask if you prepared the lamb?"

"No, it was our cook."

"That's nice."

"Yes."

"It would have been all the worse if you'd made it."

"Yes, yes."

The women relaxed into their drinks. Mme Reynard asked, "And you? I understand you've only just arrived. What have you been keeping yourself busy with? How are you?"

"I'm all right, thank you."

"What did you do today?"

"Nothing whatsoever. Yesterday I had the telephone line revitalized."

"Had it gone dead on you?"

"Yes, so I had it revitalized, and then I had a second line put in."

"Oh? What for?"

"Malcolm and I like to speak from our beds."

"Isn't that nice?"

"I suppose it is. Though I fear it may be sad. Or perhaps it's simply strange? But you should have seen the man who came to do the work of it. He was very put out by the fact of the second line."

"Was he?"

"He claimed it frivolous. When I protested he said I would have to call his superior. When I asked how I might do that without a phone he told me it wasn't his problem to solve. I pointed out that it absolutely *was* his problem to solve, though he didn't seem to understand what I meant in the moment. He was not, I don't think, the smartest telephone installer in Paris, France."

"Oh, dear."

"He finally did put in the one line, and I had him wait while I called his superior to make my case for the second. The superior asked why I should want such a thing and I told him that at a certain point each night, before sleep comes, I find myself feeling *d'humeur orageuse*."

Mme Reynard made a searching face. "You feel rainy?" she asked.

"Stormy. Then I told him that when I felt *d'humeur orageuse*, it was good for me to hear Malcolm's voice, that it comforted me. And the man, who had not been hugely friendly up to this point, suddenly softened, and he said he understood what I meant, and asked that I should put the telephone installer back on the line. The telephone installer received his reprimand and he did eventually put in the second line, but he was outraged by the loss of face and behaved with the most unsightly petulance. I tried to bring him a cup of tea but he wouldn't take it. And you should have seen the paperwork he made me fill out for him, it was thick as a dictionary."

"The French love their red tape, don't they?"

"They'd eat it on a plate if they could."

"They would, they really would."

Malcolm was bored by the conversation and excused himself to search for something to steal. Finding nothing, he moved to the kitchen to replenish his vodka. He located the bottle in the freezer; just beside this was a hefty, flesh-colored, frost-coated dildo. He stared at it a moment, then poured himself a vodka and returned to the dining room. Soon Mme Reynard excused herself to use the bathroom; in a controlled voice, Malcolm told Frances, "Go look in the freezer."

"Why?"

"Go look."

She did go look, returning in forty-five seconds with a far-away expression on her face. "I've never understood them," she said.

"What's to understand?"

"Is it something one uses alone or with someone there to help?"

"Either or."

She tapped her chin. "But why would you want it cold?"

"That's the mystery."

Frances shivered and took herself up in her arms. Mme Reynard entered the room on deliberate footsteps. The vodka had snuck up on her and she was struggling to maintain her composure. "I think I'm a little bit crocked," she said. "Malcolm, would you mind serving the cassoulet?"

"Not at all."

"I'm sure I'll scald myself if I try it. It's all ready for you in the kitchen."

Malcolm exited. Mme Reynard had a long drink of her martini. "It becomes like water, doesn't it?"

"It's better than water," said Frances.

Mme Reynard was amused by the statement. She felt very gay, because the catastrophic evening had repaired itself. She swirled her finger in her glass and stuck it in her mouth and asked, "Is it true that you've lost everything?"

"Yes," said Frances.

"And what have you got in the way of plans, if you don't mind my asking?"

"I've only just made plans last week but I don't think I should speak of them. Fresh plans—you know."

"You want to give them time to firm up?"

"Yes."

"Mustn't take them out of the oven too soon."

"That's right."

"I understand completely. You know, I don't think there's anything better for morale than fresh plans."

"Yes, I agree. I've felt so much better since I made them."

"Isn't that nice? Oh, but I wish you'd give me a hint."

"I'm sorry; I mustn't."

"I'm sure it will all come off stylishly, knowing you." She stared. "I need to make some plans myself, actually. Perhaps I'll simply copy yours, whenever they come to light."

"You could do worse."

"I'm certain I could do far worse." Mme Reynard became still, then brightened. "May I share a recollection I have of you?"

"All right."

Mme Reynard said, "It must have been twenty years ago, in the months after your husband's death. I was eating with a group at Le Cirque, and a man at my table had had dealings with your husband and was not at all enamored of him. He'd actually been speaking poorly of him when you came in. You looked so smart, I couldn't help but stare. We were all staring. As you passed the table, the man stopped you and said, 'Mrs. Price, I knew your husband well. And it's all I can do not to dance on his grave.' Do you remember it?"

"I don't, no. What did I say to him?"

"That's the thing. You didn't say a word. You drank his drink."

Frances nodded. She remembered now, distantly.

"Straight Scotch," said Mme Reynard, "and you drank it down in a gulp and then stared at him with a look of absolute indifference. You were the most beautiful woman I'd ever seen and the poor fool didn't know what to do with himself."

The women both were smiling. Frances said, "I'm sorry I was rude before. My life has fallen completely to pieces and I'm upset about it."

"I know just what you mean."

"Yes, perhaps you do, after all. Oh, look, here comes Malcolm with our dinner."

"Sustenance!" Mme Reynard cried.

# 17.

Malcolm's bedroom window looked out over a small public park. The park was unremarkable: it featured the usual number of benches, a jungle gym, a goodly amount of trees, and a border of shrubs, these favored as shelter by a rotating cast of placeless immigrants who had settled on the park as their base of operations. It was unseasonably warm for December and the park was bustling; Malcolm discovered the area could be watched in the same way a television was watched. Themes emerged, moral lessons, dramas, occasional comedies, reliable oddities. Malcolm had always been a satisfied silent observer; now he devoted a good portion of his waking moments to doing just this.

In the early mornings there came the professionals, smartly outfitted men and women cutting across the park with stern expressions on their faces. By nine o'clock the immigrants were up and mingling; by ten they had evacuated the park to roam the streets of Paris, that their human needs might be met for another day. After eleven, the park would be filled with children and their nannies, mostly African women who sat in clusters to laugh and tease and argue with one another, while the children were left to scrabble about the jungle gym. By one o'clock the nannies and children would be replaced by clerks, secretaries, and shopkeepers eating their lunches, reading books, smoking cigarettes. This group was particularly nonsocial; they were taking this time just for themselves, treasuring their solitude, their tobacco, the pull of a well-told story. In the early afternoon the nannies and children would return, the children ever more shrill and wild, the nannies calmer, the accrual of the day's fatigue rendering them duller and less joyful. The late afternoons saw all those who had crossed the park in the morning recrossing in the opposite directions. As the day wound down and the sky grew darker, the immigrants began to trickle back. At night, the park was theirs.

Days ticked by, and Malcolm saw that these routines, this schedule, had very little variation; but within its strict narrative there grew smaller stories.

Late one afternoon Malcolm watched a young woman in a black business suit enter the park and sit alone on a bench. Soon a businessman of the same age arrived and sat beside her. After a brief discussion they began kissing and petting with a passion Malcolm found indecorous, even for Paris—at a certain point the man's hand was fully inside the woman's blouse, for example. This went on for thirty or so minutes, at which point they stood, said their goodbyes, and left the park from separate exit points. This same event was reenacted the next day, and the next, and on like this so that their arrival and behaviors became a known piece of Malcolm's vista. The rigidity of their timetable, and the fact of their arriving and leaving separately, led Malcolm to understand this couple was involved in an extramarital affair.

One day they arrived at the appointed hour and sat upon the appointed bench, but now their affections were replaced by a long and seemingly unhappy discussion. The man made searching, wretched gestures with his hands; the woman began to weep. The man left, the woman remained, a cigarette smoldering in her hand but never raised to her mouth. The next day she came and sat alone on the bench. The day after this, the man came alone. The day after this the bench was empty.

Malcolm found this scenario interesting at the start but ultimately dreary in its familiarity. He preferred to follow the activity of the immigrants, which was more diverse, and so harder to define and understand.

They were all men, dark haired and olive skinned, and when Malcolm passed them in the park they spoke a language unfamiliar to him. They drank jug wine and rolled their own cigarettes and on colder nights made small, scattered fires, which lent the park a festive air; but by midnight the police would come and stomp the fires out, the embers swimming up through the dark in banking zigzags. The immigrants would be shooed away but once the police left they would return, and in the smaller hours it seemed that anything might happen.

Sometimes Malcolm saw them fighting one another, but other times the men could be seen slow-dancing to music on radios, or to the thrumming of an acoustic guitar. In his adult life, Malcolm had rarely thought of what it would be like to have male friendships; and he never pined for any. But to witness this camaraderie gave him the pang of an outlying jealousy, which embarrassed him, and which he pushed away.

He awoke at nine o'clock in the morning, as was usual for him. He rose from his bed and stood at his window. The immigrants were in various states of greeting the day, but no sign yet of the nannies and their shrieking charges. Five pigeons perched in a huddle on the branch of a sycamore at the edge of the park. Malcolm was only half watching them, but now he noticed four of the pigeons were stepping away from the fifth. They walked in a shuffling, sideways bunch while the fifth stood in place, hunkered down and shivering. After a moment it wavered and became still; then, tilting forward, it fell from the branch and plummeted beak-first through the air, thirty feet or more, crashing directly onto the belly of a sleeping immigrant. The man jumped to his feet; clutching his stomach, he studied the dead bird with the purest confusion. What dread omen was this? What woeful news was the natural world sharing with him? He looked around, desirous for a witness, someone to explain the occurrence, but there was no one, and the man snatched up his blanket and hurried from the park, the bird lying stiffly in the grass.

At this moment, the phone rang. Malcolm put the receiver to his ear and asked, "What's the opposite of a miracle?"

Frances sat upright in her bed. "How many letters?"

# 18.

Over coffee they realized it was Christmas Eve, and so they separated to buy each other presents. Malcolm bought Frances a
case of her preferred French wine; he also brought home a small
potted Christmas tree and a single string of lights. He decorated
the tree and set it on the table in the breakfast nook; he opened
one of the bottles and waited for Frances to return. When she
entered the apartment she was pushing a bicycle with a bow on
its handlebars. She had pushed it all the way up the stairwell
and was panting heavily. "Come and get it away from me, Christ,
I'm dying."

It was early evening. They drank through a first, then a second bottle of wine, and Frances became fixated on Malcolm's
lack of enthusiasm for the bicycle. Malcolm hadn't ridden a bicycle in twenty years and it was true that at first glance he was
indifferent to possess it. Frances was adamant that he should
ride it that night but Malcolm didn't want to go outside. Finally,

and thanks in part to the wine, they decided he could and should ride the bicycle in the apartment. They moved the furniture to clear a path and after two false starts he was off.

His circuit consisted of a loop in his bedroom, then down the hall and through the living room to Frances's room, another loop, and back again. The activity at the beginning required his total focus; but after a while he became more comfortable and sure of his route, and so could relax. Minutes passed with Malcolm pedaling along his path. Frances had climbed into her bed, which had been pushed to the center of her room, and Malcolm rode around her in slow circles.

"It's a smooth rider."

"Ding the bell."

He dinged the bell and went away down the hall, then returned to loop his mother. Frances was quiet. Small Frank was sitting at the foot of her bed and she was smiling at him.

"What?" Malcolm asked.

"Oh," said Frances. "I was thinking about a sailboat he bought me."

"He bought you a sailboat?"

"For Christmas one year, yes."

"Since when were you interested in sailboats?"

"I was never interested in sailboats. That's what was so curious about the gift."

"You didn't want it?"

"I didn't, no." She nudged Small Frank with her foot. Small Frank dropped his head and closed his eyes. Malcolm performed a circle in silence. He narrowly avoided crashing into a side table.

"How does a person receive a sailboat?" he asked.

"He blindfolded me and brought me to the marina. Blindfold off, he pointed out a large boat and told me it was mine. It was named *Sunny Disposish*, and it was a very nice sailboat with a teak interior and a Jacuzzi on deck and it took about six grown men to get it going." She shook her head. "He had offices in Southampton then, and had an idea that he and I would make the most of the commute. We were going to pieces for the first time and I suppose he thought a boat might return us to one another."

"It's nice that he tried."

"It's not not nice. You know what would have been nicer, though? If he'd not bought me a sailboat at all, but instead ceased fucking every lukewarm hole that crossed his field of vision."

Malcolm circled the bed twice, then rode from the room. Frances heard a rattling crash, which was the sound of Malcolm jumping from the bike and onto his bed. He hadn't eaten any dinner and was quite drunk and fell asleep almost at once; but Frances was restless, and she moved to the kitchen nook, to smoke and drink tap water, to feel her loneliness and to think of it. Small Frank had climbed onto the table, curling up at the base of the Christmas tree. In looking at its lights, Frances thought of her childhood, of her father in his robe carrying her up the stairs on Christmas Eve. He smelled of cigarettes and drink and aftershave, a combination of scents that she loved devotedly from this moment and through the span of her life. Franklin had emanated that same deadly troika when they'd met, before the alcohol had turned sour in him, and the smoke acrid.

Frances stared at the tree. She half-closed her eyes and the

Christmas lights became stretched-out spears, pulsing and tilting. She held the colored bars in her gaze; when she closed her eyes further, the lights lost their integrity, jumping to a shapeless smudge of clownish pigmentation, describing nothing, impossible to romanticize.

# 19.

Malcolm was becoming frightened of Frances. There was a furtive look about her that he couldn't name but that struck him as a manner of warning. Malcolm didn't want to be warned, he only wished to look away. The weather was fine and bright and cold all the days and weeks following Christmas, and he took to leaving after breakfast to ride his bicycle around the city. Frances missed Malcolm during these jaunts but didn't complain at his departure, as she was responsible for the new chapter in his life, the riding-a-bicycle-in-Paris chapter, and she felt the buyer's pride at having realized this for him.

In the beginning Malcolm found riding around Paris a harrowing, a genuinely frightening activity. It was not that the drivers wished to hit cyclists, as has been stated elsewhere, but it couldn't be said they were much concerned by the thought of a collision, either. It took Malcolm several days before he was comfortable traveling on primary roads; his courage grew in phases. Eventually he found himself circling the Bastille amid dense, anarchic traffic, left arm jutting out defensively as the cars and mopeds swarmed and honked at him, and the taxi drivers cursed him with lusty gusto, but ultimately all yielded rather than run Malcolm down. It was faith that enabled him to do this, faith that every hurtling vehicle would elect to stop short of killing him.

One morning he decided to go to the Buttes-Chaumont. He pedaled past the Bastille, running out of energy on Avenue Simon Bolivar and walking his bike into the park. It was eerie and unpopulated, mist clinging to the trees and bushes. Malcolm bought an ice cream from a vendor who seemed surprised at his own decision to sell frozen goods so early, and on so cold a day. Malcolm thought to warm himself by climbing to the temple, this situated on a sharply inclined island in the center of the park's small lake. He locked his bicycle to a tree and began his ascent.

The mist was burning off as he reached the summit and Malcolm stood beneath the dome of the temple watching Paris achieve visibility. He had stood in the same place with Susan, and in recalling this he suddenly missed her, after a month with hardly a thought for her. He decided he'd call and see how she'd been faring. He came down from the temple and rode along the canal. He bought a phone card from a *tabac* opposite the Gare de l'Est, then sought out a phone booth beside the water. He dialed her number and waited. Her voice was creaky: "Hello?"

"Sudsy."

"What are you doing?"

"I'm calling you. I'm calling you on the phone."

"It's five thirty in the morning."

"Ah." Malcolm snapped his fingers. "Right. I'm sorry."

Susan said nothing.

"I've just been out riding my bicycle," Malcolm said.

"What bicycle?"

"Frances bought me one for Christmas."

"That's sad. Where are you?"

"Next to the canal. Want to know what I'm looking at?"

"Not really. All right."

"Right in front of me there's a boatload of red-faced German tourists waiting for the lock to drain. Across the water there's a couple of kids playing Ping-Pong. Do you remember the solid concrete Ping-Pong tables by the canal?"

"Yes."

"They must just pour them into a mold." He paused. "I'm calling because I wanted to hear your voice," he explained.

"Here it is," she said. "Here's my voice."

But now there came another voice—a man's voice, in the background. "Who are you talking to?" it asked.

"It's Malcolm," said Susan.

"Who are you talking to?" Malcolm also asked.

"That's Tom."

Both men began asking Susan unhappy, overlapping questions.

"Wait," she said to them. "Wait a minute." She spoke to Tom first. He was displeased by the fact of Malcolm's calling, so displeased that he was leaving, he said. Susan asked him to stay but Tom said he wouldn't. Susan apologized; they made plans to discuss it at lunch. "Good luck today," she called. A quiet moment, and Susan uncovered the phone. "All right, he's gone."

Malcolm couldn't think of anything to say; he was terribly shocked and hurt to know Susan was with another man. He felt the wretched yank in his throat that signaled the possibility of tears.

"Look," said Susan, "you're not allowed even to express an opinion on the matter, do you understand me? It's beyond reason for you to try to make me feel bad about this, so don't you dare, all right?"

Malcolm nodded but didn't reply verbally.

"Were you expecting me to mourn our loss in perpetuity?" Susan asked.

"Yes," Malcolm answered truthfully. He took hold of himself. "All right," he said. "Let's hear it. Let's talk. Who is this person?"

"He was my fiancé in college. I've told you about Tom before."

Earnestly, Malcolm asked, "What were you wishing him luck for? Has he entered a dick-sucking contest?"

"That's very witty, Malcolm. No, he's got a big meeting today."

"Oh, a big meeting."

"That's right."

"Sounds big. What's this bimbo do?"

"He works on Wall Street." Preempting Malcolm's disparaging comment, Susan said, "Fuck you. At least he has a job."

"Yes, at least there's that."

"He made his own way from nothing."

"Such a hero."

Susan paused a pause which, the moment Malcolm heard it, he knew something ugly was on the other end of it. He waited for the ugliness, and here it was: "He's asked me to marry him," Susan said.

"What, again?"

"Yes."

"Why?"

"Why did he ask me to marry him?" Susan said. "Is that the question? I can only guess at that, but I assume it's to do with his wanting us to be married."

Malcolm said, "This isn't making sense to me."

"Which part?"

"All the parts. I can't imagine the scenario. Did he use the same ring as before, or is there a new ring?"

"There was no ring either time."

"That's a shame. Probably he's been too distracted by big meetings to go to the jeweler's."

"It wasn't a planned thing. It just came up yesterday."

"What, during a lull?"

"I guess so." Susan thought a moment. "You never gave me a ring either. Or is that different? I suppose you feel it's charming when you do it."

Malcolm recognized the situation was getting away from him. He decided the time had come for a bold gesture. "I want you," he said, "to come visit me in Paris."

Susan laughed, hard, and for a long time. After the laughter had passed, Malcolm said, "Well? What do you think?"

"I don't think we're through discussing what we were discussing, is what I think."

"What's to discuss? You can't accept the proposal because you're still engaged to me. It's illegal. It's polygamy."

"Malcolm?"

"That's a felony."

"Malcolm."

"What?"

"You're not allowed to behave this way. Do you understand me? It's small and cruel and I won't and don't accept it. Now, I'm sure I'm very flattered that you finally thought to call me however many weeks after your disappearance from what was our shared life. But you're mistaken if you think I'm going to welcome you back, all right? You're just wrong about it. I'm not going to do that anymore. You blew it, and it's blown, and that's all there is to it."

Malcolm's face was fixed in a portrait of concentrated discomfort. He made a sort of grunting noise.

"Listen," said Susan. "Will you—can you please not call here? At least not for a little while? I've been feeling better in the last couple of days, and I'd appreciate your keeping some distance."

Malcolm was wondering what the meanest thing he could say might be. There were so many mean things, but which was the absolute, the incontrovertible? Before he concluded his thought, however, Susan hung up the phone. He stepped from the booth, into the sunshine. The boatload of Germans was gone, as were the boys playing Ping-Pong. Malcolm drifted away from the phone booth and toward Joan's apartment. He was halfway there when he realized he'd forgotten his bicycle. He cursed and crossed the street, hailing a taxi to backtrack.

# 20.

Frances was explaining the second part of her private, two-part plan to Small Frank, and what she saw as his role in it. She spoke in terms more graphic than were necessary, perhaps, and she perceived an opposition in him. It's true that he did appear to wish to leave, but she held him fast by his middle. "Now, wait," she said. "I know. Think about what I'm saying to you, though. As if it wasn't correct." She heard Malcolm's key in the lock and turned to face the door. At the same moment Malcolm entered, Small Frank reared and bit Frances on her hand, then dashed from the apartment and down the stairwell. Malcolm inspected his mother's hand; as the bite had pierced the skin, he volunteered to visit the corner *pharmacie* for first-aid products.

The *pharmacie* was bright and white and clean and busy and Malcolm enjoyed filling his basket with every conceivable supply that Frances might need: bandages and alcohol and aspirin and topical creams. The clerk asked if he'd been hurt, and Malcolm explained about Frances and Small Frank. "At the end of the day they're still jungle creatures," the clerk said.

"Yes, and we're still apes," Malcolm told her, and he made a monkey face, scratching at his ribs.

"Oh la la," the clerk replied.

Walking back to the apartment, Malcolm spied Small Frank sitting at the edge of the park on the opposite side of the street. He crossed over to collect him but Small Frank saw him coming and ran off, darting under a bush.

Malcolm found Frances sitting on her bed, staring into space, her injured hand held to her breast. He led her to the bathroom and filled the sink with warm, soapy water. He rinsed her wounds, then dipped the cotton balls in hydrogen peroxide and wet the bite marks. Wrapping her hand in gauze, he asked, "Does that hurt?"

"No."

"Thank you."

Frances looked at Malcolm. "Why are you thanking me?" she asked.

He said he didn't know. Frances insisted they go out in search of Small Frank, and they wandered for a full two hours before rainfall forced them back indoors.

Frances couldn't sleep that night and in the morning she went out again, on her own, returning empty-handed and in a state of mounting agitation. Malcolm was unsure what he should do; that afternoon he invited over Mme Reynard to act as counsel. She brought champagne and orange juice and the three of them assembled in the living room to plot and ponder. Mme Reynard was touched to be there, and she told herself she would not leave her friends in disappointment. After some consideration, she said, "I believe we should hire a tracking dog. The dog will come here and memorize Small Frank's scent, then begin its hunt."

Malcolm had no deep faith in the scheme but thought to get behind it, if only to engage in some manner of proaction. He found a telephone directory in the kitchen and began calling around kennels and dog breeders, while Mme Reynard and Frances sat together, quietly drinking. Mme Reynard could see Frances was under considerable strain: her hair was kinked, her makeup askew, and she couldn't hold eye contact for more than a brief moment. The degradation was fascinating to Mme Reynard, but she also felt a keen sympathy for Frances.

Malcolm returned. "Failure," he said. He'd been told that locating Small Frank by smell alone was an impossibility. There were too many competing scents in Paris, and even the most gifted tracking dog could never pinpoint a single cat's location. After a tasteful pause, Mme Reynard suggested they take Small Frank's departure as a signal to welcome another animal into their lives. "A kitten is an agent of great good," she said.

Frances was shaking her head. "I didn't want a cat in the first place. I don't even *like* cats. It was only that Small Frank impressed himself upon us and there was nothing to do but endure him."

"If you feel that way, and now that he's run off, can't you simply let him go?"

"No," Frances answered. "No, no, no." She began to silently weep. She stood and left the room. Mme Reynard made herself another mimosa. "I've upset your mother," she told Malcolm.

"She's upset in a general sense," Malcolm explained. He reached for the bottle. "We're out of champagne."

Mme Reynard nodded, then looked inward for a time. "Do you ever feel," she asked, "that adulthood was thrust upon you at too young an age, and that you are still essentially a child mimicking the behaviors of the adults all around you in hopes they won't discover the meager contents of your heart?"

Malcolm was considering his answer when Frances returned from her bedroom. She looked different than when she'd left in that an answer resided in her eyes:

"The witch you fucked on the boat," she said.

# 21.

Malcolm went out for another bottle of champagne, which they drank without orange juice. Frances discussed her epiphany over a fresh, bubbling glass. "Malcolm fucked a witch on the boat over," she told Mme Reynard.

"That's nice," said Mme Reynard, and she patted Malcolm's knee.

Frances asked Malcolm, "She understood him, didn't she?"

"I think she did," Malcolm said.

"Why can't we ask her where he is?"

"I don't know that she'd know," he said doubtfully. "And I don't know where we'd find her, either."

Mme Reynard was nodding. "I would like," she said, "for one of you to explain to me just what it is you're talking about, please."

Frances said, "The fucked witch and Small Frank were connected."

"Let's not call her that," said Malcolm.

"She understood about him," Frances continued.

"Yes," Mme Reynard said, "but what *is* there to understand about Small Frank, exactly? I'm puzzled, and this is what's puzzling me."

Frances looked to Malcolm, as if to ask what she should do. Malcolm shrugged, which she took as a blessing to continue. "It's not something we typically discuss, Mme Reynard, but the long and short of it is that my dead husband lives inside that cat."

Mme Reynard's eyelid began to twitch, and she touched her hand to her face to retard this. "Is that a fact?" she asked.

"An unfortunate fact."

"And how do you know this?"

"It's an understood thing."

"Can you make it understood to me?"

"I don't know that I can. I wish you'd be good and take my word for it."

"I'll try," said Mme Reynard bravely. She was having such an exciting time, so that she could have shrieked with delight. She clamped one hand atop the other, squeezing with all her strength, telling herself to be calm.

Frances, unbidden, announced, "Small Frank ran away because I told him something he didn't like."

"Oh? And what was that?" Mme Reynard asked.

Frances shook her head. "I won't say." She looked at Malcolm. "I'm sorry but I choose not to. Anyway, I believe she might be able to help, and so we should seek her out."

"Seek out the fucked witch," said Mme Reynard.

"That's right," Frances said.

"Let's," said Malcolm, "let's think of something else to call her besides that."

Frances said, "How might we find her, is the question."

The three of them took silent sips of champagne.

"I've got it!" Mme Reynard declared, jumping to her feet and knocking the crown of her skull on the low iron lamp hanging over the coffee table. She dropped back onto the sofa, holding her head and pressing her eyes shut in pain. Through pursed lips she said, "Private investigator." She opened her eyes to study the blood painting her palm.

"I have quite a lot of first-aid products," Malcolm said, then left the room to gather these. By the time he returned, however, the volume of blood was such that the situation seemed beyond him, and he proposed they call a doctor. Mme Reynard became enthusiastic at this. She adored her physician, she said; also she was a believer in the wisdom of the phrase *the more the merrier*. Whoever could deny it as an unimpeachable truth? Frances thought she could but she elected not to, if only to save herself the trouble and time.

# 22.

Soon came Dr. Touche, a sleepy-eyed and swarthy man with the hands of a female adolescent. Mme Reynard had asked him to bring along a bottle of champagne but he'd refused, citing an aversion to it, and brought instead a bottle of Côte-de-Brouilly, which they could none of them drink, for it was corked. Dr. Touche was greatly put out by this, and he rang his wine merchant while all in the room sat watching as he described the embarrassment occasioned by the spoiled bottle. "What must these people think of me?" he asked, at which point Mme Reynard began calling out compliments. Dr. Touche waved her down, resuming his conversation: "Well?" he said. "How will you go about making this right?" He listened for a time, holding one finger aloft; now he nodded. "Yes. I think that's the only way. Do you have a pencil?" He gave the wine merchant Frances and Malcolm's address and hung up the phone. "He'll be with us shortly," he told the group.

While waiting for the merchant's arrival, Dr. Touche attended to Mme Reynard. Hers was a deep, brief puncture wound, requiring three stitches. She endured the procedure in sullen silence; once it was over, she expressed her mortification at the event. Dr. Touche had moved to the kitchen to wash up; he called out over the sound of running water: "There is nothing shameful in physical injury! The Fates have done you this damage, yet your body is already in motion to heal itself! What a wonder! What a curiosity we are!" He returned, sat beside Frances, and laid his miniature hand upon her knee. In English he asked, "What's up?" Frances removed his hand and explained in French what they had been occupied with before Mme Reynard's injury. The doctor had no visible reaction to the news of Small Frank—as—vessel but when Frances had finished, he shook his head.

"From where I stand you are in the midst of an impossibility."

"You don't believe in the supernatural?" asked Mme Reynard.

"What is there to believe in? Fear and guilt and sorrow; such motivations as these will bring us to the very strangest and most obscure places in our minds. I have no faith in this story."

"Your faith isn't required," Frances pointed out.

"Still and all. This is my opinion."

"We're going to hire a private detective to find the medium," Malcolm said.

"What an American notion."

"Thank you," said Mme Reynard. "I authored it."

A knock at the door, and now the wine merchant arrived, a gangly man with a ponytail and underarm sweat stains called Jean-Charles. He was carrying a case filled with various bottles of wine; he set this in the kitchen and began uncorking the bottles and handing out glassfuls to the guests. Regarding the offensive Côte-de-Brouilly, he explained his own buyer had recently become irresponsible in the wake of what was apparently a total mental collapse. "There is of course no excuse," he added, "but this is my truth, and you may do with it what you wish."

"What prompted the collapse?" asked Mme Reynard anxiously, as though she were concerned about the selfsame thing.

"It's a long story," said Jean-Charles, "and very little of it—indeed, none of it—makes what we like to call sense." Now he made inquiries regarding the nature of the gathering and Dr. Touche conveyed the story of Small Frank. He relished the retelling, adding minor narrative flourishes to the story that pleased him. "Sometimes, it's as if the cat were just about to open its mouth and speak." Jean-Charles seemed bored, but became alert at the mention of a private investigator; it so happened the man in the apartment opposite his was in the practice. His name was Julius, and Jean-Charles telephoned and invited him to join their group, and he accepted. The wine sampling continued as they awaited his arrival; by the time Julius appeared, none of those in attendance was sober. A glass of wine was placed in his hand by Mme Reynard; Julius thanked her but, not wanting a drink, he put the glass down. When she returned to place it back in his hand, he resignedly took a healthful sip and put the glass down a second time. Mme Reynard watched the glass. Julius couldn't deduce what she was feeling by her expression, but she did not return it to him a third time and so he supposed she was satisfied. He sat opposite the group and took out his notepad and pen.

"Who may I do what for?" he asked. He was blushing, somewhat.

Frances said, "I and my son need to find a girl, a young woman. She's a clairvoyant from the United States living somewhere in Paris. Or is she not living here but visiting, Malcolm?"

"I don't know."

"Anyway, she's around."

Julius asked, "What is your relationship to this person, madame?"

"None whatsoever." Frances pointed to Malcolm. "My son knows her carnally."

Mme Reynard began choking, and she stood and moved to the bathroom. There came the sound of gargling. In a moment she began humming to herself.

Julius told Frances, "It can be helpful for me to know the nature of your desire to find this person."

"We've lost our cat," Frances explained.

"All right."

"And this woman, we believe, might be of assistance in locating him."

"She knows its whereabouts?"

"Not at the moment, no. But I believe she can speak to the cat in her mind, if we ask her to."

Julius's pen hovered above his notepad. He opened and closed his mouth. Finally he said, "What is this woman's name?"

"Madeleine," said Frances. "We don't know her surname."

Julius asked for a physical description and Malcolm said, "She's pretty curvy, actually."

"What color is her hair?"

"Blond hair, blue eyes."

Julius wrote this down. "Do you believe Madeleine wants to

be found?" he asked. "That is, do you have any reason to believe she wants *not* to be?"

"No reason," said Frances.

The wine merchant, Jean-Charles, cleared his throat and stood and said, "I would like to share a few words." He looked away, and back. "The world changes, my friends, as the weather changes. Our motivations, our dreams and agitations, our *fears* change, too. But wine? Wine is immovable. Upon hearing good news, what do we do? We reach for wine. And when we hear bad news? Wine again."

"Gin," said Mme Reynard, reentering the room and taking up her former seat on the sofa.

Jean-Charles pretended not to hear. "I've been thirty years in the business. I give my life to wine. And wine in turn gives me life, and a livelihood. It is an honor, it is a duty, it is, yes, a calling. But where in the world would I be without my good, paying customers?" He gestured in the direction of Dr. Touche. "I would be nowhere. I would be"—he made a small space in between his thumb and forefinger—"this big. This big and no bigger. Without my good, paying customers? Well, you can just as soon forget about me. Tear me up like paper, scatter me on the breeze: termination. And that's about all I care to say about that."

Jean-Charles sat, neck aflush with emotion, moved as he was by his own words. Dr. Touche patted his friend's back and stood himself—he too wished to give a speech. He said, "We are pinned to a frozen marble boulder skating through black space at an obscene rate of speed. They say we'll soon collide with the sun, or moon, or some other passing asteroid. But

when? Perhaps today? Quite likely tomorrow. Be sure that the
end is coming, and you can take that to bed with you." He
started pacing back and forth. "My father," he continued, "when
he came home from work and it was time to take stock, would
often say, 'And how about a ribbon of wine?' Then he would un-
cork a bottle and perform a little gulp, a slip of cabernet down
the throat, a ribbon of it down the hatch, and then came relief:
'Ah,' he would say. He was a simple soul, and had no need for
art. And yet I wonder all these years later: is this wine fancy
not evidence of his love of beauty? An appreciation for fineness?
Perhaps there was a brilliance in the man, only his life didn't
allow him the latitude to locate and cultivate it. We'll never
know, alas. Dead and gone. Dead and burned and buried, pfft!"
Dr. Touche filled his glass and held it out before Jean-Charles.
"A ribbon of wine," he said.

Jean-Charles held up his glass. "A ribbon of wine."

The men clinked their glasses and drank. "Ah," they said
together. Dr. Touche sat down on the couch, looking suddenly
sorrowful, as though his own speech had made him depressed.
Julius stated his rates and Frances paid him twice what he asked
for, in cash. Folding the bills away, he said, "There isn't very
much to go on, but I'll see what I can do. I'll be in touch with
news. Or if I have no news, then I'll also be in touch. Goodbye."

"Goodbye," said Frances.

"Goodbye," said Malcolm.

"Goodbye," said Mme Reynard.

"Goodbye," said Dr. Touche.

"Goodbye," said Jean-Charles.

"Goodbye," said Julius again, and he shut the door softly
behind him.

# 23.

Julius was shy. He had always been shy, from the point of cognition down the line. Any small interaction caused him discomfort, and occasionally anguish. The post office, the market, the tailor's: the pleasure of camaraderie others derived from these moments was denied him. As a child he had been comforted when his mother explained the shyness would pass as he came of age, but it didn't pass and still had not, and then she'd died so that he could never correct her.

Curiously, his shyness did nothing to diminish his fondness for humanity. Julius loved people and was often saddened at the thought he would never truly know them. It was this shyness that brought Julius to his field of work, as he had always felt he was studying behaviors while maintaining invisibility. Why not receive a wage if he was already performing the duty? He worked only as needed and was not particularly successful, that is, not very skilled; but his mother had left him the apartment in her will, and his needs were modest, and so his life passed vaguely, evenly before him. He was in his middle years.

He was surprised by the coming of this latest job, but the cash in his pocket was thrilling. It was raining and the hole in his left shoe drank puddle water; he entered a shoe store and purchased a pair of black leather Italian loafers. This was extravagance on a level he could scarcely credit, and it served to buoy his mood, but the next morning he awoke in a state of concern at the particulars of the assignment. *A blond-haired, blue-eyed woman named Madeleine*, he thought. With such scanty clues as this, failure seemed a certainty, and he began to regret his having taken the job at all. He lingered over his hygienic rituals and afterward sat in the park, worrying and wondering if it was too late to give the money back. He felt foolish about the shoes and attempted to return them but the salesman wouldn't allow it as Julius had scuffed the soles. He slunk back to his apartment, drew the curtains, and slept. In the night he dreamed he had posted flyers describing Madeleine and that she herself had responded; after breakfast he re-created the flyers, offering a reward to the person responsible for Madeleine's unearthing. He had copies printed and all that day taped the notices up in various metro stations. Forty-eight hours later his phone rang and a hoarse voice came through the receiver claiming to know Madeleine's whereabouts. Julius was sitting up very straight; he was wearing white briefs and a pair of argyle socks. "Where is she?" he asked.

"Right here. I'm she." Madeleine coughed phlegmily. "What about this reward?"

Julius made arrangements to meet her outside the Odéon metro. They sat on the terrace of a café; Julius drank coffee,

Madeleine a double whiskey. She wore crooked sunglasses, and Kleenex peeked from her coat pockets. She wished to speak of her hardships, which were not insignificant. "The cruise line stopped payment on my check, first thing. Then I set up in a hostel but my money ran out in a week and the manager there was pure scum who rifled all the girls' bags and, I think, watched us shower through a peephole. Then my wallet was stolen, and I got fleas, or lice, and this cold." She blew her nose to illustrate. "I'm bored," she said. "I'm bored and lonely and sick and my parents won't loan me the money for a ticket home." Her head tilted. "Did that guy Malcolm put you up to this?"

"And his mother, yes."

"Are you going to give me the reward, or are they?"

"There is no reward," Julius said, and Madeleine frowned significantly. He explained about the Prices' wish to locate a missing cat, and said that perhaps there would be a fee for this service. Madeleine nodded, understanding at once what would be expected of her. She muttered something under her breath.

"What was that?" said Julius.

"I said, 'It's not like I've got anything else to do.'" She drank her whiskey down. "Take me there."

# 24.

Frances awoke to find Malcolm had gone out on his bicycle, and so she dressed and left the apartment on her own. She had begun frequenting a café nearby, but only when she was by herself. The staff called her Jackie O for her coldness, her inscrutability, her fashionable beauty. She drank red wine; she spoke to no one; she tipped lavishly, absurdly. She watched passersby on the sidewalk but never an individual, only the mass in motion. On this day she did something new, which was to fill out a postcard. Walking to the café, she'd seen two young girls sharing an elaborate farewell in the street: they shook left, then right hands; they simultaneously curtsied, cheek-kissed, twirled, and parted, smiling in affection for one another. It was a routine, a private tradition, and it put Frances in mind of Joan, hence the postcard.

She wrote: *I saw a man's penis yesterday. He was pissing in the courtyard of the apartment. Actually I've seen a number of penises since my arrival. Have you noticed men simply take them out and use them here? No harm in it, I suppose, but it takes some getting used to. Yesterday's was memorably large. What a gift that must be for a man. What a lottery life is. It was nice to see it, I'll admit.* Frances described the second part of her private, two-part plan for Joan, concluding the note with words of devotion and love. *I've always admired your heart. Your heart is the rightest of all.*

She called for the check, and in the time it took to receive it she decided she could never send the card. She folded it and left it on the table beneath her empty wineglass. The waiter found it but didn't understand English. He showed it to the other waiters and the cook but none of them knew English either. On his way home from work he stopped by the post office and mailed it. It was out of character for him to do this but he thought Frances was a special case. Recently she'd tipped him a hundred euros on a glass of house wine, and when he had protested she had said it *couldn't matter.* What did she mean by this? The waiter had mailed the card not because of the tip but because of what prompted her to leave the tip. He wasn't certain what that was, of course, only that it was something fearsome, and so, worthy of his esteem.

# 25.

Mme Reynard had, discreetly and without asking or acknowledging it, moved into the apartment with Frances and Malcolm. Each night, after long hours in close quarters, Frances or Malcolm would stand and say, "Good night, Mme Reynard," and Mme Reynard would stand as if to leave. "I hope to see you again, and soon," she'd say, "though I've so much to do. My affairs are in knots since you two came along—not that I regret it!" Standing in the open door, she'd tell them, "But yes, you'll likely see me sometime tomorrow. Pray you sleep as the dead, the dead." Malcolm and Frances would retire, and Mme Reynard would sneak to the couch to prepare her bed. Early each morning she'd leave the apartment and return to her own home to shower and change her outfit, but an hour later she'd be knocking on the door, face bright, eyes slightly demented, newspapers and croissants wrapped up in her arms. "Are you receiving?" she would ask, and they would allow her in to begin

another day together. Neither Frances nor Malcolm was bothered by this behavior, somehow. It was so thoroughly tactless
as to be fascinating to them. Frances sometimes was frightened
when she opened the freezer, but only for an instant, and her
fear was never validated.

One evening, Malcolm was sitting on the sofa eating a car-
rot and wearing for unnamed reasons a suit. Frances was yet
in her robe, and at that late hour, namely seven o'clock. She
had not left the apartment in several consecutive days and had
not taken the robe off during this time. There was a phase of
each day through which she felt conspicuous to be so attired,
specifically from when she sat down to eat her lunch and to the
moment she took her first cocktail, just preceding her dinner.
During this time she felt shabby, naked, a victim of drafts, un-
toward, and she combated such unpleasantnesses with blasts of
perfume and makeup. She knew she was living improperly but
hadn't the strength to correct herself. She had twenty thousand
euros left; she'd taken to flushing hundreds down the toilet each
morning.

Mme Reynard stood looking out the living room window.
She had been standing there fifteen minutes, and her carriage
was slack, her expression vague. Through a period of five or so
minutes, however, something caught her attention and held it.
She became increasingly alert, and finally she said, "Come look
at this, you two," and Malcolm and Frances walked over.

There was a great violence occurring in the park.

Lately there'd been an unease amid the park's inhabitants as
a new faction of immigrants had arrived and insinuated themselves into that small parcel of land. The existing group of immigrants naturally were opposed to this, and there had been

for some time an unseen line drawn down the park's center. In the day the mood was grim; in the night, when the wine and substances began to circulate, then the situation became more volatile. Malcolm had seen several skirmishes, but more recently a calm had occurred that he'd taken for peace but that was actually the prayerful moment before combat.

It was not a battle that could be praised for its intelligence; neither side could point to any strategical forethought. It was a gutter fight on a grand scale, men with grandchildren punching other men with grandchildren; piles of men; men swung about by their hair; men clawing one another's faces. It was a spectacular if grotesque sight, and Mme Reynard was pleased with herself for being the one among the trio to first take notice of it. Her friends were rapt, and all thanks to her. As such, she felt a certain ownership of the event, and she suffered an impulse to speak of it as something she was allowing them to view. "Lucky I happened to be standing in the window," she said. "We'd never have heard it otherwise." She closed, then opened her eyes. Neither Malcolm nor Frances was paying attention to her. "Close your eyes, Malcolm. You won't be able to hear it." Malcolm said, "I don't want to close my eyes." Mme Reynard felt it an ungenerous statement; in an effort to save face she began counting the immigrants, aloud but not loudly, busily, as though it were a needed thing for the benefit of all. "Fifty, roughly," she said. "Twenty-five per side." She sniffed. "It's a fair fight, anyway."

Malcolm and Frances made no comment. They'd become used to Mme Reynard's neediness and had decided the best way to curb it was to ignore her until she began behaving attractively again. Sometimes it took a while, for Mme Reynard was not unfond of self-pity, but sooner or later, thanks to time, or drink, or a restorative nap, she would return to her typical grace and good humor.

The riot swirled below them. It was no longer a demonstration of aggression performed by individuals but a unified, tidal force. Frances said, "It's becoming itself." Mme Reynard experienced an envy at these words; she knew she would never have been able to come up with something so wonderful. Hers was a mixed fate, she thought: to know brilliance on sight, but never to command it.

Riot police came pouring into the park. Abnormally large and in battlefield armor, they went about their work with authority and vigor, certain of them with an apparent pleasure. They moved through the pack knocking down the immigrants one after the other; a tap on the skull and on to the next. Soon, half the immigrants lay unconscious on the grass, while the second half had been corralled by the police and now were clustered together in a band in the center of the park. The lamplight recast the faces in masks of terrors, hatreds; blasts of hot breath shot into chill air. The immigrants had ceased fighting one another and now were waiting for what came after, a new violence. The police held shields in their left hands; they raised their clubs in their right and inched closer to the huddled men. "Look," said Frances.

One among the wounded had come to. He stood apart from the crowd, holding his head, recalling himself. Something in the grass caught his eye and he moved toward it: a billy club. He took it up and bounced it in his hand. He moved toward the policemen, who, being so focused on the group before them, were oblivious to his approach. The man selected his victim, raised his club, and swung it at a policeman's leg at the knee. The policeman dropped and the man quickly repeated the action on a second, a third policeman. Some among the officers recognized they were being attacked from behind and a small group broke away to face off against the man. A pause occurred as each side considered the other.

"Look at his face," Frances said.

The man was smiling. Blood cascaded down his face at an angle, resembling parted hair. He spit at the police; he taunted them. He menaced them with lunging motions and waved for them to advance. He was not afraid; he looked possessed, grand. Frances thought he was beautiful, and he was.

Now he attacked, and two more policemen were on the ground before the second two were atop him. They clubbed him until he was unconscious, then turned and resumed their advance upon the tightening band of immigrants. There were four smudge fires burning, one in each corner of the park; together they formed a tilting room of smoke. There was a knock on the door but no one moved to answer it. *"Entrez!"* called Mme Reynard. Julius and Madeleine let themselves into the apartment.

# 26.

They were invited to the window to watch the end of the riot.
Once it was over, Madeleine said it was a perfect ugliness, and
that police were barnyard swine. Julius posed the question of
whether or not the society of man demanded policing and rules.
Mme Reynard took up this line in sympathy but Frances cut her
off. "All police *are* swine," she declared. "That's the final fact."

Mme Reynard prepared and distributed drinks. She had,
since moving in, and in an effort to create a demand for her presence, purchased a cocktail recipe book. On this night she fixed
an antique British concoction named the Corpse Reviver II. Its
recipe called for fresh lemon, gin, Lillet, Cointreau, and a mist
of absinthe, floated with a star of anise. All were pleased with
the drink, and time passed as they discussed its history and in-
gredients. It was decided they would contact Small Frank that
night and Mme Reynard pointed out how timely it was for her
to select such a cocktail on such a day. She admitted that she'd

always wanted to take part in a séance, and that *Blithe Spirit* was her favorite movie, and had anyone seen it?

"I'm not sure this qualifies as a séance, actually," said Madeleine.

"Why not?" asked Malcolm.

"A séance is the summoning of the deceased," she replied. "I don't know if we can say that the man we're to contact is dead."

"Of course he's not dead," said Mme Reynard reassuringly.

Madeleine asked Frances, "What do you think?"

"To be honest I wish he were more dead, but I don't know if that speaks to his aliveness so much as my dislike of the man."

Madeleine looked at her with a curious expression.

"What," said Frances.

"Would you mind telling me the story?" Madeleine asked.

"Which story is that?" said Frances politely.

"How the cat came to house your husband?"

"Oh." Frances took a drink of her cocktail. "Well, he died in our bedroom one morning, you know."

"All right."

"A heart attack, and he *did* die, but it was unexpected, and I found I couldn't face it, somehow. He'd put me through such hellish trials, I can't tell you. And I was not, speaking generally, at my emotional best during this period of my life. Anyway, I was set to go away for the weekend, the car was idling in the street, the driver was loading up my luggage. And I remember thinking it was silly to tell Frank I was going, because he wouldn't care, and what was the point? But I decided I would tell him, and up the stairs I went, and he was dead in our bed, naked and uncovered, and there was a cat sitting on his chest."

"A cat or a kitten?" asked Madeleine.

"A young cat."

"Had you seen it before?"

"No. So, consider, please, the double shock of this. The corpse, but also that the corpse was being interfered with. They were mouth to mouth. The cat was licking his face and making a noise."

"What noise?"

"A wanting, almost a whining—needful. It was simply the ugliest thing, unbearable, actually, and I chased the cat away, down the stairs and out the front door. Then I went back upstairs to sit with Frank awhile. I couldn't seem to feel anything besides a sense of hopelessness, that there was nothing to be done. Then came the feeling of wishing to leave; then the feeling of needing to. The driver was honking his horn." Frances shrugged. "I left."

"Where did you go?"

"I went skiing."

"You went skiing."

"I skied."

"And you didn't tell anyone about it?"

Frances shook her head. "I don't think I said ten words the entire weekend. The story is that I was gaily vacationing, but that's not true at all. I thought of Frank all through the days, and every night I dreamed of him. He was shouting at me, but no sound came out—he was mute. Oh, he was very angry with me."

"Why?"

"I think he wanted someone to come and cover him up. To come and take care of him." Frances looked at Malcolm, who looked away. She looked back at Madeleine. "I assumed somebody else would deal with him while I was gone, but our live-in had the long weekend free, and no one else came around. I got home on Monday afternoon. The house was so quiet. When I entered our bedroom, Franklin was where I'd left him, only he was blown up like a balloon and as colorful as one, too. I called the ambulance, and the paramedics came. They were bothered by the sight of him and I suppose I must have been acting strangely, and they started in on me, asking me questions—when had I discovered him, things like that. I felt so odd, as though I wasn't completely in my own body; and I didn't think to lie to anyone. I wish I had lied, actually. It was stupid not to. The paramedics called the police and in a little while the house was full of them."

"Were you arrested?"

"Mildly. Nothing much came of it from a legal standpoint. It was the social aspects that were problematic. When I got back from the precinct the paparazzi were on the stoop, and so was the cat. It followed me in as though it were a natural thing. I knew just to look at him."

Madeleine was nodding. "All right," she said. "Let's get started and see where this wants to go." She pointed at the dining table. "Does this work for you?"

"Fine," Frances said.

"May I stay?" Mme Reynard asked Madeleine.

"Sure."

"May I?" asked Julius.

"Why not?" Madeleine turned to Malcolm. "Anyone else you want to invite over? Any neighbors or garbagemen?"

There was an *esprit de corps* among the group. Frances called for help organizing the room, and now they all began dutifully moving the furniture around.

# 27.

What had become of Franklin Price? After running away from Malcolm, he had wandered through the Marais in a state of high agitation. He had been uneasy since leaving New York City, and Frances's description of what was coming his way summed up his fears neatly. He was unsure what he should do; he only knew he could never return to her.

He walked in a northwesterly arc, eventually arriving at the Hôtel de Ville. It had begun to drizzle, and the pavement was cold on the pads of his feet. The totality of his plight revealed itself to him: to remain on the streets was to perish. As he sat under an awning watching people stream in and out of the BHV, he decided one of them would serve to save him.

He knew her when he saw her. She was a pleasant-looking, well-dressed woman in her midforties, weighed down with shopping bags. As she paused to adjust her grip, he hurried across the street to greet her. "Well, hello," she told him, then turned to go.

He had to trot to keep up; she noticed he was trailing behind, and laughed. He followed her across her courtyard and up the long flight of stairs to her apartment. She opened the door and stood looking down at Franklin. "Go on," she said, and he entered. It was as simple as that.

They spent a lazy afternoon together. She was cooking a roast and listening to talk radio. Franklin was given a bowl of milk and he drank it, then sought out a bank of light in the living room. As Franklin succumbed to sleep he felt he had found his new home, and that he would like it very much.

Unluckily for him, the woman who had welcomed him into her home was married to a man with no great regard for animals, or for anything, really, other than himself. He came home that evening in a poor mood and was looking forward to an argument with his wife. The presence of a stray cat provided a capital starting point for some first-rate viciousnesses. The sound of the husband's final bellowing assertion woke Franklin; he raised his head in time to see the man hurrying toward him. Yanking Franklin up by his neck, the husband walked him to the front door and threw him overhand down the stairwell.

Franklin was not fully conscious; it felt sickeningly alien to be soaring through the air like that. He glanced off the wall at the bottom of the stairwell and fell into a tumble, rolling clear across the vestibule. Afterward he stood at the base of the stair, livid from insult. He thought of his grander moments with a biting bitterness: his closetful of tailored suits; the scent of a limousine's heavy leathers; his belief that he was not merely a citizen of New York City but that the town was his in some fashion—the sounds were his sounds, the drawn skyline was not merely familiar, but accurate, a reflection of his ambition and achievements.

He sulked for a while, eventually curling up in the corner of the vestibule to sleep beneath a row of mailboxes. He awoke at dawn in the hands of the superintendent. The man wished Franklin no harm, but it would never do to allow strays to congregate in his building. Depositing him onto the cold concrete, he said in parting, "*Bonne chance, mon ami.*" On the contrary, Franklin's luck would only worsen.

There was a phase before the fall. He continued following women home from the BHV, but none were so friendly as the first had been. Most shooed him away at the point of recognizing his interest. One woman allowed him to spend the night, but when she caught him clawing the leg of the kitchen table in the morning she kicked him out. Another woman fed him lunch, but as soon as he'd finished she pushed him onto the landing. His mewling agitated her and she came at him with a whisk broom.

There were a number of days where he achieved not a moment of physical or mental comfort, and it became apparent that his sorry state was less a period of poor luck than something more indelible. After a sustained exposure to the elements, the indignation that accompanies placelessness must, in time, lessen. It's in this way that a down-and-outer accepts his position, but the farther down one goes, the less likely one's chance for return. Franklin was losing weight rapidly and a patch of fur was missing from his back after an evil cook had doused him with scalding oil in an alley behind a Chinese restaurant in Belleville. An ancient baseness took hold of him and he became known among the barbarous fraternity of Parisian strays as an animal deranged in his violence.

As a young man in college, Franklin had half-heartedly tried to kill himself with a bottle of Nembutal. He awoke a day and a half later and shakily went about his business, telling no one what he had done, ashamed by both the attempt and his muddling of it. In his thirties he tried a second time, with Valium, and was nearly successful, but his secretary discovered him sprawled on the floor of his office after hours. Paramedics revived him and he claimed it an accidental overdose. The secretary thought this was untrue; Franklin gave her a large bonus, which she took rightly as her cue to maintain silence on the matter.

Now, in his feline incarnation, Franklin once more knew the need for death. There was no other solution, he was certain; one morning he set out to achieve his exit.

He spent several hours walking the streets of Paris. His method of departure was yet unknown; he considered his options. Might he dash under the tires of a city bus? Throw himself into the Seine? In the shadow of the Eiffel Tower, he cleaned himself. Looking up at that behemoth structure, he realized he'd arrived at the location of his own demise.

In the past, whenever he'd heard of someone jumping to his death, Franklin had been sickened by the thought of it: the plummet, the rendezvous with concrete. Who could desire such a sheer end as that? But now he understood it. The pavement was an immovable solution to the larger problem, and the pavement could not be mishandled or botched. Furthermore, his desire for death was so vigorous as to summon in him a wish for his vessel to be annihilated. Franklin Price wanted to explode.

He began his ascent, climbing the three hundred sixty stairs to the first level of the tower, nearly two hundred feet from the ground; this was the only place from which one might jump with a clear line to the ground. He lapped the platform several times. From the western side he looked down at the Champ-de-Mars, its expansive, placid field of trimmed green grass. From the east, he studied the Seine, clogged with the tiered Bateaux-Mouches, open-air boats transporting tourists up and down the river. He stepped past the safety barriers and to the edge of the platform. Peering down, the wind in his ears, he had no God to curse or plead with, and there was no one he wished to seek out or consider.

He stepped into the air and dropped, headfirst. Craning his neck, he witnessed the ground's approach. He closed his eyes in anticipation of impact but at the moment just preceding this he involuntarily righted himself, landing squarely on his paws. A moment passed before Franklin understood he hadn't died. He was shaking, and his paws smarted from the force of impact, but he wasn't dead—no, not even injured.

Incredulous, he climbed the steps a second time. Rushing to the platform's edge, he leapt out as far as he was able, and all through the descent his only thought was of self-control, of the connection of skull to pavement. But as before, and at the final moment, he spun about to land upright. Franklin Price learned that an animal cannot commit suicide, this due to its survival instinct, which overrides emotion and will. He limped away from the tower, taking bitter solace in the thought that he would likely die from malnutrition in the near future.

He wandered through the afternoon and into the night. He was curled up beneath a darkened merry-go-round across from the Voltaire metro station, waiting for sleep to come, when a queer force gripped and fixed his consciousness. A voice was coming at him, then voices; they were not heard but known from somewhere within him. They wished to speak with him, and he found he couldn't help but acquiesce. He dipped toward a trance; his mind was warm.

# 28.

"Hello?" said Madeleine. "We're here with you, Franklin. Won't you please speak with us?"

The group sat in a circle around the dining room table, staring at a candle placed at the center of their wheel. When Franklin's voice arrived, the flame bowed; it seemed he was transmitting from the light itself:

"Who are you?" he asked.

"My name's Madeleine. We met on the trip over, do you remember?"

"What do you want?"

"Just to speak with you."

"What about?"

"Yourself. I'm here with Frances and Malcolm. Maybe you'd like to say hello to them?"

Franklin was silent.

"Hello, Frank," said Frances.

"Hello."

"How are you?"

"Oh, you know. You're there with Malcolm?"

"That's right."

"Malcolm?"

"Yeah, Dad."

"What's this all about?"

"All what, Dad?"

"The hocus-pocus."

"Just that you ran off, you know."

"Yes?"

"And we were curious about where you'd gone to."

"No one place," said Franklin. "I'm behaving nomadically."

"Are you in- or outdoors?"

"Out."

"Aren't you cold?"

"I am."

"Are you hungry?"

"A lot of the time."

"What do you do all day?"

"Not much. Walk around."

"You're living by your wits," said Mme Reynard. "I admire that."

Franklin paused. "Who said that?"

"Mme Reynard is my name, and I'm so very happy to meet you. I'm a great friend of your wife and son. Honestly, they've had the most remarkable influence over me. I believe friendship is a greater force for good than any religion ever was, don't you agree?"

"I've never thought of it before," Franklin said.

"Think of it now, and I'm sure you'll come to see it my way. And I can tell you that Frances and Malcolm have been worried sick, actually sick—worried to the point of illness—about you."

Franklin said, "Frances, who is this person?"

"She just told you who she is, Frank."

"*Reynard*," Mme Reynard repeated. "Can you not hear us well?"

"I can hear you."

"Well, I want you to know that I think of you already as a friend. I have friendly feelings toward you, and I hope that we can become just as close as I already am with your fine, fine family. I find your plight ever so fascinating, and I have so many questions I want to ask you. For example: do you think cat thoughts or man thoughts?"

"Frances," said Franklin.

"Have you fallen in with a mad cast of plucky, down-at-heel characters?"

"Frances, please."

Frances patted Mme Reynard's hand to quiet her, but she either didn't comprehend the hint or chose to ignore it: "Is there love in the dingy back streets? I would imagine one's senses become all the more acute under such duress, and romance must seem doubly significant. Think of the phenomenon of the procreation boom just after a war. It's the human spirit standing its ground, saying, in effect: I will not be repressed. It's actually quite moving, if you take a moment to ponder it." She looked about the table to see what effect her words had had on her friends but there was none, or, if there was, it was subdued to the point of imperceptibility.

Malcolm asked, "Why'd you run away, Dad?"

"Good question. Great question. Why don't you ask your mother why?"

Malcolm asked Frances, "Why did Dad run away?"

Frances said, "It's pretty complicated."

Franklin said, "It's not *that* complicated."

Frances was staring at the candle; its light was quivering in her eyes. "Where are you, Frank?" she asked.

"I choose not to answer that," said Franklin. "Does anyone want to know why?"

"I do," said Mme Reynard.

"Me too," said Madeleine.

"I do and I don't," Malcolm said.

Franklin said, "It's just the small matter of Frances's intention to kill me with her bare hands."

All in the room looked at Frances, whose noble bearing held for some moments, but soon toppled as she sputtered, cackling madly. The sound startled Julius, so that he spilled his wineglass onto the tablecloth. "I'm sorry! Excuse me!" He was mortified with himself; he hurried into the kitchen in search of a towel.

"All right, who's *that?*" Franklin asked.

"Julius is his name," said Mme Reynard. "I don't know him very well but I have a good feeling about him. He's been so helpful and chivalrous." When Julius returned, towel in hand, she told him, "Say hello to Franklin."

"Hello," said Julius softly, face burning as he mopped up the wine.

Mme Reynard said, "Julius cuts a romantic figure: the man in the night, seeking. He's after answers, information. It must be a terribly rewarding job, Julius, is it?"

Julius bobbed his head back and forth.

"But to have a *quest*," said Mme Reynard. "That's what I find most enviable. My life has been utterly questless. And I'm very sorry to say it, I can tell you that."

"Sorry, what's his quest?" Franklin asked.

Julius briefly explained his role in the story.

"And Frances pays you for this? Frances?"

"What?"

"You pay this joker a fee?"

"Don't be rude, Frank."

"And what about this Madeleine? What's her take?"

"Shut up, Frank."

"Hey, Julius?" said Franklin.

Julius was still working to remove the wine stain. "Yes?" he said.

"You found this Madeleine, who's now found me, is that right?"

"Right."

"Then what are you still hanging around for? If your work's already done?"

Julius said, "I asked to stay . . . I wanted to see . . ." The wine wasn't coming up at all. "Do you have any soda water?" he whispered to Frances, who shrugged.

"Frances?" said Franklin. "Listen to me."

"All right."

"Listen to what I'm telling you, Frances."

"I'm listening, Frank."

"These people? Your new buddies? They're charlatans. They're pretending they don't know each other when in fact they're working in tandem to con you."

"Well, that's just silly."

"I'll tell you what's silly. You want to know what's silly? I'll tell you, if you want to know."

"You simply don't know what you're talking about. Julius and Madeleine are both lovely people, and they've been so helpful, and I'm very happy to've made their acquaintance." She raised her glass in tribute to her new friends. Mme Reynard tugged Frances's sleeve; she too wished to be complimented. Frances said, "And you, dear." Mme Reynard beamed.

"Fine," said Franklin. "Let them have it all. What do I care? But don't say I didn't warn you." He paused. "Why do I suddenly feel like I'm the punch line to a drinking game? What do you people *want*?"

"You know what I want, Frank. I've gone to some length to locate you and I find your refusal to come home perfectly vulgar. I never asked you for anything in my life and now I want this one thing from you."

"One little thing."

"I've earned it."

"How?"

"I could have done *anything*," said Frances. "I could have been *anything*. I gave you my life and you turned it into bad television."

"I made you rich."

"I was already rich."

"Running on fumes when I met you."

"Anyway, the money's all gone—"

"Whose fault is that?"

"—the money's all gone and I want you, I *demand* that you come home and accept what's owed you."

"Yeah, well, I'll check with my secretary and get back to you. Hey, Malcolm?"

"Yes, Dad?"

"What do you think of all this?"

"All of what?"

"Your mother wants to kill your father."

"Yeah."

"Any thoughts on it?" said Franklin.

"To be honest, I'd just as soon not get involved."

"Nice. That's nice. That's family for you."

Malcolm made a funny face. He cleared his throat. "I guess what I really mean to say, Dad, is: I don't know that it's fair for you to ask me to weigh in on something so personal as this considering the fact that I don't know who you are, have never known who you are, and not because I didn't want to but because you never so much as parted the curtain for me, never showed me the slightest preference or kindness, even as a child when I worshipped you and all I ever wished for was for you to take me by the hand and walk me through any motherfucking park, pat me on the fucking head, for Christ's sake was I that repellent a creature to you?" Malcolm stood and hurled his cocktail glass against the wall. It exploded and he stalked out, slamming the door to his bedroom.

"What's eating him?" asked Franklin.

"He just told you what's eating him, Frank. He hates you." Frances was patting her hair to sculpt it.

"Right," said Franklin. "Right. Well, it's been great catching up with you, Frances, but I think I'm going to go back to starving to death, if no one objects."

Mme Reynard objected. She had, she said, more questions than time would apparently allow, and would have to accept that the bulk would remain unanswered, but before he rang off, she asked that Franklin humor her, and share with the assembled an overall summation of the experience of becoming a cat. Franklin sighed as he considered his answer. "On the whole it's been frustrating, I guess is the word."

"How is it frustrating?"

"Well, I have all my old thoughts and desires but I can't do anything about them. I miss being alive, as a man. I enjoyed it."

"You always seemed so angry to me," said Frances.

"I was. But I loved being angry."

"You did not."

"I absolutely did. That's something nonangry people never give angry people credit for. It's fun, being mad. I loved my work. I loved the game of it. I loved money. I loved getting away with everything."

Frances told him, "But you didn't get away with it, did you?"

"I got away with a lot. More than most, anyway."

"Yes, but look at you now."

Franklin was silent for a while. The candle flame flapped, then pulled itself taut. "Fuck you," he said, and the flame snuffed itself, and all at the table sat contemplating the drift of smoke.

# 29.

Malcolm and Frances left the apartment early the next morning. In wandering, they found themselves at the natural history museum. They took in the exhibits together, then separated to roam alone. At one point Malcolm stood on the fourth floor, leaning on the railing and watching his mother sitting at the café on the second floor. She was unaware of his spying on her. What he felt was love and fear; he was panicked to keep her close by. He went to the toilet to wash his face; written on the wall beside the mirror were the words, *Caesar sees her: "Seizure, seize her."* This bothered Malcolm. He lately had been feeling that the world was showing him more than the needed amount of unpleasantness. He moved to the café and sat across from Frances.

"I'm homesick," she declared.

"For the apartment?"

"No."

Malcolm said, "Well, I'm ready to go back to New York if you are."

Frances was disturbed by this; she realized Malcolm didn't understand what she, what they were doing in Paris. "Oh, pal," was all she could think to say. She had given Madeleine five thousand euros for her services, and another three to Julius as a bonus. She had nine thousand euros to her name; she wondered how she might get rid of it.

They returned home, with little said between them. As they walked through the park, Frances noticed the man who had been so courageous in the riot sitting on a bench eating an orange from a mesh sack. His face was welted and decorated with multicolored bruises, but he didn't appear unhappy. He smiled at Frances, who, for the first time in she could not recall how long, turned away in shyness.

Mme Reynard received them at the door. "I don't like it when you go away without warning," she told them. "It makes me feel so alone, so vulnerable."

"Take it easy—take a bus," said Frances, and she honked Mme Reynard's nose. She placed a chair at the window to watch the man on the bench, while Malcolm lay on the couch reading a French tabloid. Mme Reynard had made a soufflé, and this soon was served. After eating, Frances bathed, dressed, and made up her face. In her room she folded seven thousand euros into her coat pocket and left the apartment without telling Mme Reynard or Malcolm.

The man was still sitting on the bench. Sunlight banked off his battered face; his eyes were closed. Frances sat beside him and he turned to look at her, greeting her as *la femme à la fenêtre*—the woman in the window. Frances nodded and he offered her an orange and she declined. He apologized for the state of his face. "Normally, I'm quite handsome, and not just my friends would say it."

"I'm sure that's the truth," she said.

"Rest assured. And know I shall be handsome again."

Frances was smiling. She said, "I saw what happened last night."

"Is that right? Well, well. It was a big show, anyway. What did you make of it?"

"Just that I thought you behaved very bravely."

The man dipped his head bashfully; but, he was also proud. He expressed a regret for the manner, the style of his violence. "But you must understand that for a man in my position, the police are the lowest forms of life, and so I afford them nothing like respect, nothing but the worst parts of me, which is all they deserve."

Frances explained her own dislike of police, and the man held his hand solemnly to his heart. She asked why he wasn't in jail and he said, "They held us in a line just up the street beside the river. The man in charge of us was distracted, he kept looking away, and finally he walked off and out of sight, as though we were just going to sit there and wait for him to come back. The strange thing is that everyone did, except for me."

"Weren't you handcuffed?"

"I was, but look." He displayed his wrists, which were wrapped in bruising and burst blood vessels. "Thick wrists. It was the same way with your Billy the Kid. You know Billy the Kid?"

"I know him."

"He always got away and I always get away, too."

Frances said she had changed her mind about the orange, and the man became lively in his search. "Only the finest orange for you, madame," he said. "The finest, the most delectable orange in this sack? That is the orange you will receive on this day, for you are my guest, the mysterious, the beautiful woman in the window." He located the winning orange and peeled it on her behalf. "Hold out your hand," he instructed, and she did, and he laid the sphere in the dell of her palm. Gravely, he asked, "May I have some of your orange, please, madame?"

They shared the orange. It was a pleasant moment for the both of them, and they were happy to've met. When the orange was gone, she passed the man the seven thousand euros. He held the bills in his hand.

"I'm very ill," she told him.

He studied her doubtfully. "You don't look ill."

"I am. I haven't very long to live, if you want to know the truth. So, you see, you'd be doing me a great favor to accept this. It would help me."

"How would it help you?"

"It would make me happy."

In a clarifying tone, he said, "Is there anything you want me to *do* for this money?"

"Not at all."

The man thought for a while. He peeled off a thousand euros, then handed the rest back to Frances.

"Won't you take it all?"

"No." He pointed to another immigrant sitting close by, at the base of a tree. The man was obviously very drunk, and looked to possess less than the average quantity of intelligence. "That man there? He'll take the rest of the money."

The man on the bench stood and hefted his sack of oranges over his shoulder. He held out his free hand and Frances gave him hers. Bowing, he drifted away from the park and moved toward the river. After he'd gone, Frances walked over to the man sitting under the tree. She proffered the money and he took it in his fist and stood. He said nothing to Frances; he walked off in the same direction the man on the bench had.

Frances watched the man disappear. She did not have the feeling she'd hoped for. She looked up at the apartment and saw that Malcolm was watching her. She waved; he didn't.

# 30.

Julius returned in the morning with a discreet overnight bag and a book. Mme Reynard welcomed him in and he sat on the sofa waiting for someone to question his being there. When no one did, he opened the book and started reading. In a little while Mme Reynard set a bowl of strawberries on the coffee table and he ate them.

Madeleine arrived before lunch, struggling under the weight of her duffel bag. "Where's Malcolm's room?" she asked Julius, and Julius pointed, then resumed his reading. Madeleine found Malcolm sitting up in bed, shirtless. She said, "Look, I need to stay here for a little while. Is that okay?"

"Yes," said Malcolm. And, "Hello, how are you?"

"Fine. I'll be flying home in a couple days." She hefted her bag onto the bed. "I'm not going to fuck you, Malcolm, all right? Things are weird enough as is."

"Okay."

"Actually I think it's pretty weird we fucked in the first place."

"I'm comfortable not talking about it," Malcolm said.

Madeleine unzipped her bag. "I need a drawer."

Malcolm pointed to the armoire, then put on his robe and moved to the living room to sit beside Julius. Mme Reynard emerged from the kitchen wearing a colorful cooking smock and carrying a soup-filled spoon, which she held out for Malcolm to taste. "More salt I think," he said, and she returned to the kitchen. Joan let herself into the apartment, pale as paper, key in trembling hand. "Where's Frances?" she demanded. "In the bath," said Malcolm. Joan dropped her bags and hurried down the hall. Finding the bathroom door locked she frantically knocked; when Frances called out, Joan went half to pieces. Malcolm led her by the arm to the couch; over the sound of her sobbing, he asked, "How've you been, Joan?" Soon Frances exited the bathroom seeking to comfort her friend. Joan had been worried, now was relieved, but soon became angry, then forgiving, and at last, very jolly and glad. She and Frances began making plans for the afternoon, plans that did not include Mme Reynard, who stood nearby looking stricken, disturbed as she was by Joan's appearance. Pulling up a chair, she asked how long Joan might be staying in Paris.

"I can't be sure," said Joan. She had a kindly but puzzled expression on her face. "May I ask who you are?"

"Mme Reynard is my name."

"How do you do?"

"I do better than people give me credit for. How do *you* do?"

Joan looked to Frances, who was smiling, then back to Mme Reynard, who was not. Mme Reynard didn't like the way Joan was sitting on the couch. "Do you know where you'll be staying? It can be difficult finding a hotel room at the last minute."

"This is my own apartment," Joan replied. Mme Reynard shrugged, as though in doubt of the statement's veracity. She returned to the kitchen to clang pots and plateware in protest. Joan followed Frances to the bedroom.

"Who is this horrible woman in my home?"

"Isn't she a riot?"

"I don't think she is a riot, no."

"Give her a chance, she isn't so bad."

"Since when do you humor your admirers?"

"It's strange, isn't it? I've adopted an attitude of pure passivity, it seems. Perhaps I'm simply tired. Yes, I think that's what it is."

"And the postcard?" said Joan.

Frances stated her mystification at the fact of its being sent. Joan explained she was not interested in the riddle of the note's delivery so much as its contents.

"A low day," Frances explained. "And the mood has passed."

"Has it?" Joan asked.

Frances took Joan's hand and kissed it. "Yes, dear."

They lunched. Joan complimented Mme Reynard's soup, which mollified the woman somewhat. Julius, whom Joan hadn't fully noticed earlier, introduced himself; then Madeleine emerged from Malcolm's room, rubbing her eyes. "I fell asleep," she announced. To Joan, she asked, "What's your name?"

Joan turned to Frances. "Ballpark figure. How many people are living here?"

"This is everyone," Frances assured her friend. But Susan arrived an hour after, with her fiancé Tom in tow. As they set their suitcases down, Frances said, "All right, but *this* is everyone, I promise."

# 31.

Tom's foremost characteristic was his handsomeness; his second was his normality; his third was his absolute lack of humor; his fourth, his inability to be embarrassed. He addressed the group at the dinner table: "I'm sorry for the intrusion. But I don't know what else I could have done, to be honest. I'm in a very painful situation at the moment. I hope you all can understand."

"Oh no," said Mme Reynard, chewing, "what's the matter?"

"In short, I'm in love with Susan."

"Is that so bad a thing, taken altogether?"

"It would be cause for celebration if the love were returned."

"Is it not returned?" Mme Reynard covered her eyes. "I can't bear it."

Tom became wistful. "Before I met Susan I thought I knew what it was to be in love. I had said it and meant it. I'd heard it

said to me, and been so glad to know. But what were those feelings, compared to this? This is something else. This is the love
the poets aspire to."

"Are you a poet?" asked Mme Reynard.

"I work in finance. There is, I feel, a sort of poetry in num-
bers."

Malcolm said quietly, "Gross."

"What did you say?" asked Tom.

"I said, gross."

Tom watched Malcolm with a plain face, then refocused on
Mme Reynard. "I asked Susan to marry me twice. Once in college, and she says thanks but no thanks. But then the second
time around she says, you know what? Let's do it."

"Isn't that lovely?" said Mme Reynard.

"Anyway it was. And we were both so happy. Then she gets
this late-night phone call. She won't so much as paraphrase the
conversation, but from the moment she hung up the phone I've
been playing catch-up trying to figure out just what it is she wants.
And if I'm not mistaken, what she wants is him." Tom pointed at
Malcolm.

Mme Reynard was thoroughly immersed in the story. She
asked Susan, "What do you have to say about all this?"

"It's like Tom says. I thought I was happy. I *was* happy. But
then Malcolm called and now I don't know what I'm doing." She
turned to Malcolm. "What am I doing?" she asked, but Malcolm only shrugged. "I wonder," she said, "if you can take your
head out of your ass for just the briefest moment."

Tom said, "I don't think it's necessary that we succumb to
our animal selves, here. It's a complicated situation but I believe

we can express our respective points of view while maintaining our dignity."

"Bravo," said Mme Reynard.

"Which isn't to say we should hide our emotions."

"Oh, never."

"For example, I feel that I could kill Malcolm," said Tom, shifting in his seat. "Actually murder him, here and now." A phase of quiet occurred where all at the table took in Tom as a physical specimen. He was over six feet tall and powerfully built. "Here and now," he repeated. "After all, if he wasn't around, wouldn't my problems all be solved?"

"They would," said Mme Reynard sympathetically. "They really would."

"But no, I won't do that," Tom said, looking away from Malcolm and down at his plateful of shrimp.

"You're lucky," Mme Reynard told Malcolm.

"I've always been lucky," Malcolm told her.

"Have you?"

"No, I was being droll."

Mme Reynard thought a moment. "I've been neither lucky nor unlucky," she said. "I've been luckless—such a bore."

Frances said, "I've been incredibly lucky at times, but tragically unlucky at others."

Madeleine said, "I've only been unlucky but I have a sense this'll change at some point, suddenly and permanently. Anyway, that's what I tell myself."

Julius said, "I've only been unlucky and I believe I'll always be."

"Where am I going to sleep?" Susan asked, looking around the apartment.

"Where are *we* going to sleep," Tom said.

After dinner, Joan pulled a foam mattress from the crawl space. It accommodated but one body; Tom volunteered to sleep on the floor. He affected the noble attitude of one enduring discomfort for a greater cause and he bore it insufferably and everyone disliked him except for Mme Reynard.

Julius slept beside Mme Reynard on the couch, which was a foldout, she was delighted to discover. Tapping her chin, she warned Julius, "I talk in my sleep."

"That's all right."

"Also I gnash my teeth."

"All right."

"And I have sleep apnea, and sometimes I sleepwalk. If you see me set out to wander you mustn't wake me. But if I try to leave the apartment, will you guide me back around?"

"Okay."

Mme Reynard became sheepish. "Occasionally I suffer from nightsickness," she admitted.

"What's nightsickness?"

"I sometimes—rarely—vomit the bed."

Julius said, "Sweet dreams, Mme Reynard."

"I never do dream," she lamented. "Oh, life!"

Joan and Frances lay together in their pajamas. They smelled of gin and cold cream and Frances whispered giddily, "We're just two little old ladies!" Their laughter was muffled in the pillows; they were so glad to be reunited.

With the coming of Susan, Malcolm felt uneasy sleeping beside Madeleine, and he had a thought to check her into a hotel, but after his bath he found her sleeping soundly in pajamas; and in considering her gentle face he saw nothing improper in sharing a bed with her. He was cautious not to wake her as he climbed under the duvet cover. When she stole the duvet away, he put his jacket on back to front and slept with his knees pulled up to his chest.

Sleep took the group, and silence enveloped the apartment.

# 32.

Frances did something peculiar. It was deep in the night and she awoke from a panicked dream of suffocation death. She stood away from her bed, then left the room and paused in the hall, listening. Moving to the front door, she slipped her coat and shoes on, exited the apartment, and began walking. Other than the rare passing scooter or taxi she was alone in the streets. She walked for ten minutes and found herself standing beneath what until recently had been her own apartment. The light in her bedroom was on, curiously, but only her light; the rest of the building was dim. From the sidewalk she could see that the walls were naked, artworks removed, and a fresh coat of paint had already been applied. It hurt her to think of her effects and artifacts stacked in crates in a darkened underground storage facility somewhere. They would be sold in bulk, at auction, to a buyer who did not know her, and so could not be worthy to possess them.

From the side of her eye she saw a dark figure, head and neck merely suggested, moving along the bottom right-hand corner of the bedroom window, then dipping out of sight. She knew that it was only a painter or real estate agent or someone from the bank, but the very idea that someone was there while she was not, and that she was barred from entering, made her miserable. When the bedroom went black, Frances turned away and walked in the direction of Joan's apartment.

Stepping down a narrow, lampless passageway, a man in the distance was walking toward her on the sidewalk. He wore a long coat and cap and he was, she noticed, audibly reproaching an unknown antagonist with great bitterness, even hatred. Frances assumed the man to be one among the long-suffering and placeless individuals who roamed city streets at night, unfortunate people driven across the brink by, she supposed, an absence of comforts; but in coming closer to him, she saw that his clothing was not at all shabby, and that his face was shaved, his hair tidy and trimmed. When he noticed her approach he abruptly ceased walking, ceased talking. She looked down as she passed him; he rotated to watch her stepping by. She was six paces out when he asked her, "Are you all right, madame?"

Frances stopped and turned. The man had a pleasant, healthy face. He'd been so angry only a moment before, but now he looked and was acting as a gentleman. "Why wouldn't I be?" she asked.

"Just that it's quite late to be out."

"You are."

"Yes, that's true," said the man. "Well, good night." The man touched the brim of his hat and took a step away from Frances.

"I've lost my cat," she said.

The man paused. He studied Frances more closely. "Yes,

you have the look of someone who has," he said. "And that's why you're out so late?"

"That's right," she said.

"Would you like me to help you look?"

"Oh, no thank you."

The man thought. "Have you checked under the bed?"

Frances shook her head.

The man said, "Everything I've ever lost in my life has always wound up being under the bed."

"I'll look when I get home," said Frances.

He turned again and walked off and Frances stared after him but said nothing more. She wondered who he'd been cursing with such passion. *He's going home to her now,* she thought, smiling.

She returned to Joan's apartment. It was very warm inside and her hands felt pinpricked. She stood in the vestibule, warming them, and her mind was wandering in a pleasing way. Now she did the peculiar thing. She stepped across the room to stand over Tom and Susan, to watch their sleeping faces. Susan's was undeniably fine, and Frances couldn't help but admire her unblemished cheek and neck. Next she studied Tom. He looked stupid even in slumber, Frances thought. When she looked back at Susan, Susan's eyes were open, and she said to Frances, "Hello."

"Oh, hello," Frances answered.

"What are you doing?"

"Just, you know, up and around."

"What?"

"I'm just walking around." She scissored her fingers back and forth to mimic a stepping gait.

Susan stretched her arms. "You're not planning on killing me, I hope?"

"No," said Frances.

"Oh, that's good." There was a pause. "Do you want me to get up and keep you company?"

"No, I don't want that."

"Okay. Well, I guess I'll try to go back to sleep."

"All right," said Frances. "Good night." She returned to her room. She was blushing as she crawled into bed, and she thought, *What did I do that for?* She was almost asleep when she recalled what the man in the street had said. Hanging upside down, she checked under the bed, but there was nothing there.

# 33.

A party was the decorous thing, it was decided. Frances and Joan went out after breakfast for supplies, having received a list from Mme Reynard, who to her credit did not ask to come along but stayed behind to ready the kitchen for cooking, and the apartment for entertaining. Frances had two thousand euros left and was intent on spending every cent at La Grande Épicerie. This was apparent to Joan, and she became suspicious. "Saffron isn't on the list."

"Saffron is a necessity."

"Three bottles of saffron."

"We'll use it later or sooner."

Frances began loading caviar into the cart. Joan volunteered to pay the bill but Frances said it wasn't necessary, it was all budgeted out.

"Dutch," Joan said.

"No, I have to spend it all."

"Why?"

"You're *supposed* to spend it all. That's the object of the game."
She sent Joan away to seek out the cheese; after she'd gone,
Frances called over the wine clerk. "Give me something worth
five hundred."

"Case or a bottle?"

"Bottle."

She had a moment of dread at the checkout when she realized there were twenty euros left over. But then she saw a sign
beside the cashier explaining that all groceries could be delivered for just that amount, and so she wrote down Joan's address
and handed over the last of the money and she felt greatly unburdened, even proud in some way. She took Joan by the arm
and proposed they walk home. Passing through a park, they
saw a man and woman lying in the grass, kissing passionately.
Frances asked, "Do you and Don still make love?"

"Every year on his birthday."

"But not *your* birthday."

"Just a nice dinner for me, thank you. Sometimes we go
again around Easter."

Frances lit a cigarette. "Do you regret not having children?"

"Never once. Never for a day. Do you regret having one?"

Frances laughed.

"I'm being serious," said Joan.

"Oh. Well, sometimes I do, to be honest."

"But you wouldn't change him."

"Yes, I would."

"But you wouldn't change him much."

"I'd change him quite a bit."

"But you love him."

"So much that it pains me."

Joan reached for Frances's cigarette, took a drag, and handed it back. "What do you make of this Susan?" she asked.

Frances made a grim face. "No tactical intelligence whatsoever."

"I'm sympathetic. I don't think it would be very easy to love Malcolm."

"It's easy enough."

"Don't be such a hard case. She's sweet."

"What's that worth?"

"Something, I think."

Frances said, "I don't want to talk about her."

Joan held up her hands in truce. "Moving right along," she said. "When was the last time *you* made love?"

"You know perfectly well that it's been years. I had a close call on the way over." Here Frances told the story of the ship's captain; by the end of it, Joan was laughing her loud American laugh.

She asked, "How do you feel when you look back on your romantic exploits?"

"A little bit embarrassed, actually," Frances said.

"Really?"

"I blew half the ambulatory men in Manhattan."

"I hope you don't regret it?"

"There's very little I regret."

"Such as what?"

"You want me to tell you what I regret?"

"Yes."

"Well, I'm not going to."

They crossed the Seine. Joan was smiling to herself about

something. She said, "I told Don I had to run to Paris because I thought you were going to kill yourself. He was fiddling with the television remote and he told me, 'Tell her hello, if you get there in time.'"

This amused rather than offended Frances. "Don never was a deep feeler."

"That's true. But I'm not even criticizing him. To be honest, I've come to appreciate the way he is. I had a moment earlier this year where I realized that I am, at the base of it, happy, and that Don and I have fulfilled what we set out to fulfill for each other. Can you understand how shocking this was for me?"

"Shocking because you shouldn't be satisfied with what you've got?"

She shook her head. "You get older and you don't even want love. Not the love we believed in when we were young. Who has the energy for that? I mean, when I think of the way we used to carry on about it."

"I know."

"Men and women throwing themselves out of windows." She paused. "What you want is to know someone's there; you also want them to leave you alone. I've got that with Don. But, I was shocked because I suddenly understood that the heart takes care of itself. We allow ourselves contentment; our heart brings us ease in its good time."

"It's a nice thought," said Frances.

"You don't agree?"

Frances flicked her cigarette away. "It hasn't been my experience."

# 34.

They found themselves on the border of the Tuileries garden. "Look where we are," said Joan. "Do you want to go to the Louvre?"

"Fuck the Louvre."

"D'Orsay?"

Frances nodded, though she didn't much care to go. Taxiing back over the Seine, she felt a magnet pull in her stomach. It was as if the water wanted her, and she waited in dread for the feeling to pass, and it did pass once the taxi cleared the river. Joan paid the driver and then the museum admission. The Musée d'Orsay was nearly empty. From the moment they entered, Joan's mood changed; she became sullen and withdrawn. Frances asked her what was the matter and after a stuttering start Joan expressed contempt for the suicide note, the idea of suicide from a woman such as Frances, the cliché of someone so bright and promising killing herself once the glamour has passed.

"Well, for one," said Frances, "that's an extremely shitty thing to say to me. Two, the glamour passed a long time ago, and you know very well that it did. And third, three, yes, my life is riddled by clichés, but do you know what a cliché is? It's a story so fine and thrilling that it's grown old in its hopeful retelling."

Joan couldn't help but smile at this.

"People tell it," Frances said. "Not so many live it."

# 35.

In the late afternoon the group assembled for cocktails. Without consorting about it they'd all dressed up, and the women's perfumes fought for supremacy in the living room. The sun set, candles were lit; Mme Reynard found an English dictionary among the cookbooks and proposed they play the game called Dictionary, whereby a player assigns an incorrect definition to an unknown word in hopes of fooling the other players.

She claimed the secateur was the saboteur's assistant, Malcolm that costalgia was a shared reminiscence, Susan that a remotion was a lateral promotion, Frances that polonaise was an outmoded British condiment fabricated from a horse's bone marrow, Madeleine that a puncheon was a contentious luncheon, and Joan that a syrt was a Syrian breath mint. Julius, whose English was not fully matured, said that unbearing was the act of "removing a bear from a peopled premises." Tom proposed that a raptorial was a lesson on forcible intercourse and was so roundly berated for this that he quit the game and sat to the side of the group in a sulk, muttering bitterly that language was for communication, not obfuscation. "I feel uneasy when things don't make sense," he admitted.

The game wound down and dinner was served, a roast, and a salad of watercress, rocket, and Roquefort, then dessert, a *charlotte Malakoff au chocolat* much admired by the partygoers, which brought Mme Reynard a flush of pleasure. "Say what you want about Julia. I know some will drag her through the mud, but in the end, what are they actually accomplishing with this? Defining their own limitations, defending a sparse arsenal. I give credit where it's due, and I'll thank you to do the same."

"Who is Julia?" Tom whispered to Joan.

"Child."

Tom misunderstood. He turned to Susan and asked, "Who is Julia?"

Frances surprised the group and herself by volunteering to wash the dishes. She had performed the chore perhaps six times in her life and so the movements were both familiar and faraway. It was such a simple action, yet it felt almost religious, a gesture acknowledging something larger, more enduring than oneself. Malcolm dried and stacked, working efficiently but without his mother's enthusiasm. Actually he was bothered by Frances's taking up the task. It was so far from her typical behavior as to indicate the approach of peril.

In leaving and then returning to the party, Frances and Malcolm sensed a shift in the air. All were drunk, as were they; all were continuing to drink with no thought to stop. Tom and Julius were quietly, earnestly arm wrestling at the dining room table. On the couch, Susan and Madeleine were trying to explain to Mme Reynard that there was no bad blood between them, a concept Mme Reynard couldn't seem to grasp. "I can't claim to know either of you well, or at all, but I can see you're above such petty jealousies. Ugliness begets ugliness. I volunteer we strive for grace."

"Neither of us is bothered, Mme Reynard," Susan said.

"You *say* that, but you obviously don't mean it."

"But I'm not in love with Malcolm," Madeleine said. "To be honest, I don't even like him very much."

"I'm comfortable not talking about it," Malcolm said, pulling up a chair.

"Oh, why can't we all be friends?" Mme Reynard asked. Her lips began to quiver and she burst into tears.

"We've upset Mme Reynard," Susan told Madeleine.

Madeleine patted Mme Reynard on the back. "Please don't cry. Your makeup's going to run—and there's so much of it."

There came a thud in the background as Tom defeated Julius. Now he challenged Malcolm, who had had enough to drink that it seemed a sound idea. He moved to sit at the dining room table; Julius declared himself officiator: "Ready? Steady? Go!" he said, and Tom slammed Malcolm's hand down on the tabletop. Malcolm had offered not the slightest resistance. "You win," he said.

"Come on," said Tom. "Do it right."

Malcolm nodded and they clasped hands. Julius set them off, and again Tom won effortlessly. "You're the big winner," Malcolm told him.

"It's not winning if you win like that," Tom complained. "He's not even trying."

The women drifted over. Joan and Frances walked side by

side, linked at the arm; Mme Reynard was dabbing her eyes and giving thanks for Madeleine and Susan's heartening encouragements. Malcolm looked up at Susan's pretty, drunk face. He felt he loved her very much and told Tom, "If I win, you take your bag and leave—alone." Tom's expression grew steely, and for the third time the men joined hands. Julius set them off and Tom let out a war cry as he brought Malcolm's hand crashing down on the tabletop. Malcolm hadn't tried at all; Tom, panting, asked, "Wait a minute. What do I win?"

"Nothing," said Malcolm. "Everything is exactly the same as before."

Mme Reynard said, "This reminds me of the performance artist I saw on the television. She walked the length of the Great Wall of China, then broke up with her boyfriend, then everyone paid good money to watch her go to the bathroom in a bucket in a museum."

Malcolm was absently rubbing his smarting knuckles. Susan knelt beside him and took up his hand in hers. She drew his hand to her mouth and kissed it. Tom stood apart from the group and said, "I don't like you people." He turned to Susan. "I don't like these people. They're not normal people."

Mme Reynard took hold of Tom by his shoulders. "Tom, I speak for the group when I say that I've enjoyed, so very much, meeting and talking with you. Couldn't you please find it in your heart to like us just a little bit?"

"No."

Mme Reynard sat on the sofa. "I tried and failed—but tried."

Now Julius faced Tom. Swaying, he opened, then closed his mouth. He stood breathing from his nose awhile. "I'm not used to drinking this much," he said, and also sat down on the sofa.

Malcolm stood before Tom. "Tom," he said, and Tom drew back and punched him in the nose. Malcolm fell-sat back down, hand covering his face and nodding, as though the violence against him was just, even commonsensible.

Frances slapped Tom in the face, then sat down herself.

Tom stood there looking woebegone. "I'm leaving," he told Susan. "Are you coming with me or not?"

"I'm not," she said, smiling at Malcolm, who wore a jaunty mustache of blood.

"This is your last chance."

"I'm not coming."

"It's now or never, Susan."

"Never, please, thank you."

Tom collected his baggage and left the apartment in a state of mortification and bafflement. Mme Reynard took this as a cue to refresh everyone's drinks. "Well," she said, "we're down a man; one of our group has defected. But perhaps the lack will bring those remaining nearer together?" They raised their glasses and drank to the thought.

Malcolm led Susan away from the group and to his bedroom, closing the door behind them. He drew back his sleeve to remove his watch, which Susan recognized as her father's, and which she hadn't known he still possessed. He put it on her wrist and began tightening the band for her. "I asked you to come and you came," he said. He was attentive to the act of putting on the watch. Susan laid her free hand on his face. "You're dripping blood on my sweater, honey."

# 36.

Now came strangenesses. After Malcolm and Susan reemerged, Mme Reynard announced it was time for a talent show, and though none much wished to take part, her enthusiasm outweighed their disinclination. She began, by reciting a number of Emily Dickinson poems she knew by heart: "How happy is the little stone, that rambles in the road alone." She spoke from her deeper self and all were impressed by her memory, and how the words affected her. She was near tears when she said,

"I sing to use the waiting
"My bonnet but to tie
"And shut the door unto my house;
"No more to do have I,
"Till, his best step approaching,
"We journey to the day,

"And tell each other how we sang
"To keep the dark away."

There was lively applause as Mme Reynard sat, mildly quaking, eyes gleaming with the gratification of the performer in triumph.

Joan elected to go next. She fetched a sheaf of loose paper and pencil. "Name something and I'll draw it."

Mme Reynard said, "Draw me."

Joan quickly and expertly drew Mme Reynard. In the portrait she was as in life, sitting on the sofa with a drink in her hand, forward leaning, an affable yet mildly psychotic look in her eye. But it was not an unflattering likeness, and as the drawing was passed from hand to hand, a great many compliments were afforded Joan. Mme Reynard set the drawing safely to the side, saying she would cherish it always. She was straining to hold her head upright.

Julius stood to address the group. He said, "I've been sitting here wondering what I can share with you, but I can't think of a single thing. This is embarrassing for me, as you can imagine, but I want you to know how much I've been enjoying myself here. Thank you for allowing me to sit in your company. I hope that I may continue to do so. That's all." He bowed and sat, and there was among the guests a heartening chatter, statements of fondness for the reticent PI. Julius translated the mood and was moved by it. Though he had not entertained anyone, he'd gone through the same emotional transfiguration as the entertainer, and he experienced an uncommon sense of fulfillment.

Frances stood, drink in hand. She was going to tell a story, she said.

"Is it a happy story?" Mme Reynard asked.

"No," Frances said.

"What's it about?"

"It's about the time I set my parents' house on fire."

"Well," said Mme Reynard.

"I've heard this before," Joan said. "It's a good one."

The group waited. Frances sipped her gin and began. "My mother one day decided she hated me, and she was not adept at hiding this; in fact she had no thought to hide it; in further fact, she wished to share it. Her method was to ignore me, to such an extent that I now can only wonder at her sanity. I'm not saying she was averse to me—that she would avoid me. I'm saying she began to live her life as though I did not and had never existed. I would greet her and she would pretend I wasn't there at all. She looked not at but through me. If I persisted in speaking to her she would leave the room, or the house.

"This went on for many months, and had what I believe was the desired result, which was for me to doubt the truth of my own existence. I was ten years old, eleven. Once I overheard my father pleading with her to address me, and she said sadly, 'I'm sorry, darling, but I can't do that, and I won't.' She couldn't reconcile herself to aging and she disliked that I was favored by my father. I outshone her. That's really all there was to it. She wanted to send me away but Father wouldn't allow it, so her ignoring me was her revenge, and it was brilliant in its effectiveness." Frances took another drink. "There were bright spots in my life. My governess, Olivia, and I were close, then, and Father was always kind, and sympathetic. But Olivia could only do so much, and Father was gone half the time, more than half the time; at some point each day I would see my mother but she wouldn't see me and it began to damage me.

"Well, a birthday of mine occurred, and of course my mother did not bring me a gift, or attend my party, which was at our own house. Late that night I lay in my bed, surrounded by my presents and cards, and I was taken up by the most unpleasant, the most violent desperation. It was too great a feeling to bury; I had to act. I decided to set the house on fire. I should say I had no wish for Mother to burn, but I knew she would *react*, and this was my dream.

"Olivia was sleeping, and Mother was, and Father was out of town. I took a stick of kindling from the firebox in my room and stuck it in the glowing ashes of the hearth until it caught fire. I touched the flame to the curtains. Once they were alight, I went to tell Mother. I still had the smoldering kindling in my hand; I held it near her face and she woke up hacking. Her face was very frightful and ugly and when she sat up I told her, 'Mother I've set my room on fire.' She said nothing. 'My room's on fire, Mother,' I said. Still she said nothing to me, but after a moment she rose from bed, rang the fire department, dressed, and quickly left the house. I watched from her window as she drove off into the night.

"Olivia was screaming, now. Her room was just to the side of mine, and the smoke woke her up. I returned to my room and found her batting at the wall of fire with my duvet cover. Poor Olivia, she was so frightened. I could hear the sirens, but they were a long way off, like a mosquito near your ear.

"The first thing the firemen did was kick down the front

door, which was unlocked, and nowhere near the fire upstairs. Then they kicked down all the other doors, took axes to the house, and coated every inch of the interior with their fire hoses. Oil paintings blasted from the walls; statues toppled from the pedestals. It was the most thorough act of vandalism I'll ever witness, I'm certain of it. Standing amid the hissing wreckage, the commissioner later explained that fire was the most insistent and insidious of the four elements, and that you could show it no mercy—which was fine, but the estate was destroyed, more or less. It took the whole summer and into the fall to restore it to its former state and it was years before it lost its smoky scent.

"I can remember listening to Olivia speaking with my mother on the telephone. Mother had driven to the airport and was waiting to board a flight for the Bahamas. Olivia said, 'It's one thing to care for a child, quite another to sleep across the hall from an arsonist. I'm not saying I won't do it, but we're going to need to discuss my wage.' She listened awhile, then hung up, clapped her hands, and told me we were going to stay in a hotel, and that food would be brought to our rooms, and the television would be bright and loud, and there would be a pool for swimming and pastries with tea every afternoon. All these things were true."

"But what happened to you?" asked Mme Reynard.

"Just that. We moved into a suite at the Four Seasons. I had the time of my life. There were no repercussions that I can recall. My mother remained in the Bahamas for the season. My father sent a psychiatrist to the hotel to speak with me. He asked why I'd done it and I told him and he said he understood and went away. That's the story of my setting my childhood home on fire."

Frances sat, and the group discussed the story. Mme Reynard said she enjoyed the tale as it provided an insight into Frances's character, but it was ultimately unfulfilling in that there was no punishment rendered for what was a very serious, even an evil deed. Julius said it reminded him of *Gone with the Wind*, though he had never seen *Gone with the Wind*, but he had a sense that there was a narrative sameness occurring. Mme Reynard told him that beyond the fact of each story featuring a house fire he was wrong, but that Julius should see *Gone with the Wind* the first chance he got, as it was a classic that withstood what she called the very terrible test of time.

Now came Madeleine's turn, only she, like Julius, had no talent to share, she claimed; she asked if she could be excused from the exercise and was told she could not. "Can't we count the séance as my turn?" she said. The answer: no. "Well, can I just tell a story, too?" she asked, and it was granted she could, and she decided she would explain how it was she'd come to her line of work.

She said, "When I was eight years old I was sitting in the kitchen eating a bowl of cereal and my grandma walked into the room, and she was lime green. It clung to her skin but bled away when she moved, like a mist coming off her. I asked her what was the matter and she said, 'Nothing, why?' In a little while she said she was tired, and she went to lie down, and she closed her eyes and died. I didn't tell anyone about it. A year later I saw a green man at the supermarket. I broke away from my mom to follow him at a distance, up and down the aisles. I followed him through the checkout and to the parking lot. He sat in his truck, turned it on, then off. He started jerking around in his seat. Foam was coming out of his mouth. I watched him die in his truck. A cop came, and I told him and my mom about the man's greenness, and my grandma's. The cop told my mom to take me to a hospital and she did, and a doctor heard me out, then put me under observation—three days and nights in a padded room. After that I pretended I couldn't see the greenness anymore."

"But you could," said Mme Reynard.

"I could and still can."

"Am I green?"

"You're pink."

"Hmm," said Mme Reynard. She suggested that Madeleine should work in the medical field. "Think of all the lives you could save."

Madeleine shook her head. "The greenness isn't a signal that someone's in danger of dying," she explained, "it's that they're going to."

Malcolm was made uncomfortable by the subject matter and decided the time had come for him to share his talent. He stood and performed a sleight-of-hand trick that gave the impression his thumb was detaching from, then reattaching to, his hand. The group found this wanting, and it was asked that he should give them something more dynamic. Mme Reynard encouraged him to tell a story, as Frances and Madeleine had. "What kind of story do you want to hear?" he asked.

"Sad and scary," she replied immediately.

Malcolm stood awhile, gazing back in time, combing through his own particulars.

# 37.

When Malcolm was ten years old he got word his mother and father would not be hosting him at home that summer, and that he would spend the coming months at the academy. The headmaster told him as much, in his oak-paneled chambers, and it was this typically domineering man's observable discomfort in sharing the news rather than the news itself that encouraged in Malcolm a true dread. This was doubled when the headmaster explained, in as casual a tone as he could manage, that the extent of Malcolm's society would be the assistant headmistress, a clammy stoic with a paste of hair across her weirdly miniature forehead, and the groundsman, known to the children as the Moss Man, as he looked like a creature just emerging from moss-covered swamp waters.

The headmaster exited the room. Malcolm sat wondering what the man had been paid to allow for what was doubtless an oversight of academy protocol—likely a good amount, he thought. The assistant headmistress and groundsman were given less, or none, judging by their displeasure at his presence. The three of them took their first meal that night: a rubble pile of unpeeled, unseasoned potatoes, lukewarm liver, and a glass of tap water. The assistant headmistress and groundsman were having an argument in pantomime, each trying to get the other to explain something to Malcolm. At last the assistant head-mistress told him, "Meals are at nine, one, and seven. We won't come looking for you if you don't show up." She glanced at the groundsman and back. "Neither of us is going to watch after you. We've got our own work to do. Do you understand?"

Malcolm nodded. There was a silence.

The groundsman told him, "Just so long as you understand that."

The academy was situated in a remote section of the Ad-irondacks. The experience of walking through the halls without another student around was momentarily thrilling for Mal-colm, but as the sun began setting, and the shadows grew longer on the walls, then did the dread return to him. Night came, a proper night, and it was awful to lie in the dormitory with all the empty beds. He had never felt so exposed, so perfectly killable. He demanded sleep of himself, and sleep came, and he woke at dawn to pace the grounds, the sun low, full, and blazing. Having attended the academy for several years, he knew the surround-ing terrain well, for miles in each direction, but it was different now that he was on his own, and he would only venture to the edge of the nearby forest, keeping the academy within sight, a short sprint to safety. In recent months Malcolm had found his thoughts shifting from the benignly strange to the grotesquely sexual and apocalyptic. He supposed this meant he was growing up, but he didn't want to grow up. Adulthood had no benefits that he could see and he was loath to join that cruel population.

The assistant headmistress and groundsman did not warm to Malcolm. Actually they resented him increasingly as the days passed by, and though Malcolm tried to win their favor, this always went badly: in clearing the table he dropped a dish; in pouring out water he missed the groundsman's mug. After such attempts, Malcolm disliked himself. When he realized the shame made him feel worse than their silence and meanness did, he quit trying, and simply endured.

There was one meal that stood out as comparably pleasant. The assistant headmistress and groundsman were laughing together when he entered, and the woman half-smiled at him and said, "Here he is, ready to feed," a foreign civility that made Malcolm blush. The meal was more elaborate than the rest had been: roast chicken and vegetables, mashed potatoes, milk rather than tap water, and a lopsided chocolate cake for dessert. Malcolm ate it all, ogling the assistant headmistress and groundsman, who were drinking wine and chatting away as though nothing had ever been the matter. He wondered at the nature of the friendliness that had come between them. It made him wince to think of them in romantic embrace, but still, this new scenario was preferable to the other. Unfortunately, in the morning the chill had returned to the table, and the food was once more merely edible. The assistant headmistress and groundsman were hungover, and the friendliness was gone.

Malcolm's days grew interminable, his boredom so acute he felt he could scream, or slap his own face. He had never once taken up a book for pleasure but now passed dense hours reading novels curled up on the deep-brown velvet couch in the librarian's office. The librarian was named Ms. Roach, and the boys all loved her because she was quietly kind and would tell no secrets of herself. Malcolm inspected her work space for something personally illuminative but he found nothing, every drawer clean as a pin. He had the sense Ms. Roach enjoyed her work there, and so he too was pleased to be passing time in her office. But he soon came to learn that books were not the solution in entirety. They were about life, but they were not life itself, and he closed them up and put them away. Summer break was two-thirds passed.

One night at dinner, the assistant headmistress was more terse with Malcolm than usual, and when the groundsman left for his postmeal cigarette she clamped him at the arm. "Let go," he said. But she gripped him tighter still, pinching the tendon in his small bicep. There was not an anger in her eyes, but fear; she was trying to tell him something terrible, he realized. "He's not well," was how she phrased it.

Malcolm understood. "All right."

"Keep clear of him," she said.

The assistant headmistress and groundsman had had an alliance, but it was soured, and now the groundsman treated her with contempt; and she was increasingly afraid of him. Rather than endure the quiet at mealtimes, Malcolm took to fasting, so that he often became dizzy from hunger. He slept long hours to kill away the days, but unhappy dreams pursued him. His father was an occasional extra, an opaque man crossing a room in the background. He dreamed of his mother more frequently, and in overvivid color, and she was sweet, and doting, and curious— always pleased to be near him.

One morning the Moss Man sat alone at the breakfast table,

gnawing a piece of bread and drinking black coffee from a dirty wineglass. Malcolm was very hungry but there was nothing prepared for him. "She's gone off," the Moss Man said.

"When's she coming back?" Malcolm asked.

"Not ever." The Moss Man went away, to lie beneath the tractor in the field. He spent whole days at this. Sometimes he did seem to be working toward fixing the tractor but more often he was only dozing, drunk on port wine. Malcolm watched him from the library; when the Moss Man's feet hadn't stirred in hours he went outside and crept close enough that he could hear a low gurgle of venom coming from the man—he was lying under the broken tractor hissing unkindnesses. Malcolm thought something had gone wrong inside the Moss Man.

Late in the night he woke to find the Moss Man standing at the foot of his bed, in a slack, stained T-shirt, swaying in place, and his hands were fists and Malcolm told him, "Please go away," and the Moss Man did go away. But all through the night Malcolm could hear him smashing glass and howling from corners of the cavernous building. It was quiet in the morning and Malcolm knew enough to leave. There was no food in the kitchen besides wilted carrots and a bottle of wine, and he took these, along with his toothbrush and a Jules Verne compendium, all in a sack, and he walked in what he believed was a southward direction, because he knew there was a town to the south. Actually he was walking to the north. Not that it mattered in the end.

Malcolm understood that he was having an adventure. He was running away from the academy and he felt bold on the one hand, but unsure if he was a match for the outsize task. A nervous shiver took him up as he set out, but after a mile the shiver eased. At two miles he was untroubled. At five miles he stopped walking and ate the carrots. It hadn't occurred to him to pack a corkscrew so he couldn't open the wine; he flung it down a steep, forested incline. It fell and fell and when it finally disappeared it made no sound, which was at once heartbreaking and divine.

His sack was lighter, with nothing in it except for the book and toothbrush, and he was following a logging road and it was warmer now, the sun directly overhead. Why hadn't he brought a hat? Wait: why hadn't he brought a blanket? Why hadn't he brought a knife, or matches? It was too far to turn back, and he knew he couldn't face the Moss Man again. He walked on; it was so hot the ground was ticking. When his flesh began to burn he steered into the forest, which was slower going but shadier. He spoke to his mother, imagining the scenario of his showing up at the door of their home in Manhattan. He would say, "No, I didn't like it at the academy. There was a bad man there and I was very bored without my friends to talk to." He tried to think of some *interesting things* to say to her. This was what he believed his mother craved the most, for a person to say *interesting things*. He came up with nothing but he felt hopeful the interesting things would materialize when he truly needed them.

An hour passed and he began to sense he wasn't alone. At first this was an abstract fear; but then he heard a *knock!* in the distance at his back. He stopped walking, listening over the drumming of his heartbeat. He hadn't imagined it, there it was again: *knock—knock!* It was the sound of wood on wood, a club on the trunk of a tree, he thought. He knew that it was the Moss Man in pursuit of him, toying with him. He quickened his pace but now he worried the Moss Man was close by at his heels, or possibly to either side of him, even in front of him. The Moss Man was omniscient, and Malcolm was lost, and the afternoon was passing and he wished he'd stayed on the logging road, with a clear view a mile in each direction and the occasional fleck of trash in the bushes, a comforting reminder of civilization. It began to grow dark and he was sure that at any moment the Moss Man's great hand would dart from behind a tree, catch his hair, and drag him off to an unspeakable end. He started running. He ran until he couldn't, and he hunched over, spitting foam and heaving. He ran again and stopped again. He ran again and found a bowed river and drank from it. The river cheered him somewhat because it afforded a plan, a route of escape: should the Moss Man appear, he would jump in the water and be off.

He walked downriver and soon came upon a campsite situated on a grassy ledge up from the water. A boy his own age stood beside a large canvas army tent; as soon as he saw Malcolm, he ducked under the flap and a moment later a family of six poured out: a mother, father, two sons, two daughters. The mother asked him, "What's the matter, honey? Are you lost?" And Malcolm, knowing he was finally safe, became hysterical.

As an adult he would remember: the mustiness of the tent, and that he ate four hot dogs in a row, and that one of the daughters was pretty, friendly, and unafraid. She wore a silver crucifix necklace and a Nike half shirt and she touched his face in the tent and said, *Don't worry, Martin, we're nice,* and Malcolm loved her. But none of what happened after—how he found his way back to the academy, what became of the family, or the assistant headmistress, or the Moss Man—was recoverable.

## 38.

The tale received high praises from everyone except for Madeleine, who had passed out, and Frances, who said the story made her feel villainous. Malcolm said he'd never thought of her as even remotely villainous and that while, yes, she had been a slow starter, she'd more than made up for it later. She accepted this, or appeared to accept it, and now the group had one last drink—the drink they would regret in the morning. They were silent for this event. There was nothing the matter; everyone was happy, satisfied. But a tiredness had come over them, and they eased into their fatigue, comfortable enough with one another to let it show.

Frances stood and bowed to the group to wish them good night. She asked Malcolm, "Walk me home?" and he led her to her room. She seemed nervous, fidgeting and tugging at her hair. Malcolm asked her what was wrong and she admitted she was bothered by the thought of his hating his father.

"Since when?" he asked.

"Since now."

"Why now?"

"I don't like you carrying that around with you. Also, I don't quite feel your father warrants it."

"This coming from the person who wants to strangle him."

"Yes, but my offense is greater than yours. My wanting to kill him is due to his prior kindnesses."

Malcolm said, "What does that mean?"

"I want to kill him for destroying what was a very perfect story of love," she explained. "But in your case, his being absent was in your interest and he knew it was. He'd destroyed himself by the time you came around, and you were better off not knowing him at all."

"All right." Malcolm paused. "Can I ask you a very dramatic question?"

"Yes."

"Why did you have me in the first place?"

Frances raised her eyebrows. "That *is* dramatic."

"I know. And I'm sorry. But why did you?"

"It wasn't planned, of course. As far as I knew I couldn't have children, and I'd never much wanted any before that. Then when it happened, we thought your presence could help us come together. You were a last-ditch effort, in effect. But then, when he saw you, it clarified something for him, and he turned away forever, from you and me both."

"But I shouldn't hate him," said Malcolm.

"You can and maybe it's inevitable but I'm telling you it's a waste of your own time and that by hating him you're only empowering him and giving him more credit than he deserves. Your father is an emotional moron, but he isn't evil."

Malcolm had a searching look on his face. "What happened when you saw me?"

Frances said, "I've never been so hurt by something in my life as when I saw your face for the first time. And I asked them to take you away, because I felt I'd die if they didn't."

"Why?" Malcolm asked.

"Reasons," she said. "Because you were your father. Because you were me. Because we were all three of us so ruinous."

"And why did you come to me when you did?"

Frances brightened. "That was strange, wasn't it?"

"It was unexpected."

"What did you think of my showing up like that?"

"Well, I wanted you to come, you know. But I'd wanted you to come for so long that when you finally did, I was confused."

"I'm sorry."

"Don't be. I was happy, really."

"Were you?"

"Yes."

Frances studied Malcolm with an expression of sly fondness. "I hadn't known you were you. I'd have come right away, if I had. I'd never have let you go in the first place." She said, "You understand what it did for me?"

"Yes."

"Do you?"

"Yes."

"I hope you do."

"I do."

"I love you, pal."

"I love you, too."

She kissed him lightly on the cheek and dropped into bed.

There was something in her physicality that made Malcolm see his mother as a young girl. She lay still, facedown, and Malcolm exited the room, closing the door behind him. Susan was standing in the doorway of their bedroom, smiling as she waited for him. Behind her, in the living room, Julius and Mme Reynard were moving Madeleine from the couch to the foam pad on the floor, the both of them laughing but trying to laugh quietly so as not to wake her. Joan was in the kitchen rinsing the cocktail glasses. Malcolm felt happy in this moment. As he entered his room he called to his friends, "Good night," and "Good night," his friends replied.

## 39.

Hours passed; the apartment was still. Susan couldn't sleep and she snuck from Malcolm's room to the kitchen to make herself a cup of tea. She found Frances there, standing in the dark, smoking. "Oh, hello," Susan said.

"Hello," Frances answered.

Susan filled the kettle. She noticed that Frances had changed into a red cocktail dress, and she asked, "What are you doing?"

"Just what it looks like."

"Can't you sleep either?"

"I can sleep."

Susan put the kettle on the stovetop. Frances stubbed out her cigarette and lit another: *click!* The women had nothing to say to each other and Susan dreaded the silence. Just to make a sound, she said, "I don't know Paris very well." Frances merely looked at her. "I want to know it," she added, and Frances made a sweeping motion toward the window, in the style of the game-show beauty summing up a stageful of glittering riches. The gesture said that the city was Susan's for the knowing, but it also implied something more critical, an accusation of stupidity or helplessness. Susan thought, *I won't say another word to her. I'll make my tea and leave without a good night, even.* But then Frances's face softened, and she spoke in a tone Susan had never heard, no longer arch, but candid, and without spite.

"I came here all the time when I was your age, and younger. It was the thing to do, for certain of our generation, and I loved it in a way that took me by surprise—startled me, actually. Even the decay was elegant. And I felt anonymous, as if all the consequences of Manhattan society were irrelevant. I had a secondary life here, which was needed, and good.

"Once I was married, then I began to come with Malcolm's father. It was different in a way I couldn't define for a while, then I realized he'd ruined it for me."

"Ruined it how?"

"The simple fact of his being."

"He didn't like it here?"

"He did, somewhat, but that's not what I mean. With Franklin here I was no longer anonymous, and he was the reasonable voice I'd been free of. He inhibited the way I walked, dressed, the way I spoke, everything."

"All right."

"So, I stopped coming here, blaming the city: it had changed, it was spoiled. I put Paris out of my mind. But then Franklin died, and now it was me and Malcolm. He heard me speak French to a waiter in New York one day, which made him curious, so much that we came here together, and I could see him having the same reaction I'd had when I was young."

"He liked it?"

"Very much. I taught him how to order a croissant in French, and he went to the patisserie every morning on his own, and was so proud of his efficiency. His first knowledge of worldliness. Then when we came home he asked for French lessons, and it wasn't very long before he had it down. We started visiting Paris together. We bought an apartment. I'd become enamored of the place again, through him." Frances drew from her cigarette. This was the end of the story, apparently.

"How do you feel about Paris now?" Susan asked.

"I still love it here, but I feel that I've been forced to return, which I resent." She stubbed out her cigarette and lit another. The kettle whined and Susan turned the stove off. She was very tired; also she was still drunk. The combined effect was a sense of calm confidence, and she found herself asking, "Why are you always so vicious to me, Frances?"

"Because you want to take him away."

Susan opened her mouth to argue against this but then she thought, *That's true.* "All right," she said, "but what if you're getting in the way of his happiness?"

"He's happy with me."

This too was true.

"I don't like myself when I'm around you," Frances added. "I don't like the way I behave, which of course is my own fault, but in the end it's just another reason to disapprove of you." This was said in such a way as to represent an olive branch. Susan felt a smile growing across her face.

"I can't win, then," she said.

"No," said Frances. "You can't. But perhaps that doesn't matter so much."

Susan told Frances it did matter and that she knew it did.

Frances said, "Perhaps it will matter less soon."

The next day, Susan told this story to Malcolm: "All of a sudden she said, 'Here, let me help you,' and she took over making my tea. As she handed me the cup, she asked if you were asleep and I said you were. She said that if I drank the tea—she'd picked valerian root—I'd fall right to sleep, too. I told her I hoped she was right and she said, 'Go to sleep, Susan.' She sent me away but stayed in the kitchen, standing in that same stiff way as before, arms crossed, smoking in the dark in her cocktail dress with the price tag still hanging off the hem."

# 40.

"Madeleine, wake up," Frances whispered.

"What?"

"Wake up."

Madeleine opened her eyes. It was after four o'clock in the morning and Frances was richly, vividly green. She explained that she wanted to speak with Franklin again. Madeleine was feeling ill from the gin and asked if they could contact him in the morning, but Frances was insistent, and she pulled Madeleine up and led her to the bathroom. She had a candle prepared, the lights already dimmed. Madeleine splashed water on her face. Sitting cross-legged on the tile countertop, she communicated with the candle flame, which presently began its flickering.

"Hello, what?" said Franklin.

"Hello, Frank," said Frances. "I'm sorry to bother you again. Were you sleeping?"

"No."

"What were you doing?"

"Just sitting here, under this bench."

"I see. Well, I was just thinking of you, you know. So I thought I'd give you a ring."

Franklin said nothing.

"Don't you want to know what I was thinking about?" asked Frances.

"All right," Franklin said.

"It's three things, actually. Number one is: do you remember our first date?"

"I don't, no."

"Yes, you do. You took me to Tavern on the Green."

"I don't remember, Frances."

"You *do*, Frank. You ate your cupcake with a fork and knife. No?"

"No."

"You surely did do it." Frances was amused at the memory. "*Why* did you do that?" she asked. "With the fork and knife, I mean. What were you trying to pass yourself off as?"

"I don't know, Frances," he said peevishly. "Who knows?"

Frances took a deep breath. "The second thing I want to talk to you about is that I feel badly about our last conversation, and I wanted you to know I don't hate you anymore." When Franklin failed to respond, Frances asked him, "Perhaps you have a reaction to that news, that you'd care to share?"

Franklin said, "It's late to be telling me this."

"Late in the night, or late in life?"

"Both, but mainly late in life."

"I can't understand that as an attitude," Frances admitted.

"Your wife of long years, who only days earlier wanted to murder you, has experienced a sudden and mysterious shift in feeling for the good. Is that not noteworthy?"

"I guess so, but Frances?"

"Yes?"

"I'm a cat."

"I know that."

"I'm a cat living under a bench, and it's raining, and I've got fleas, and, you know, I'm not much concerned about anything else besides the unhappy facts of my horrible—my truly horrible, miserable fucking existence."

"I see," said Frances. "Well, whether or not you care to know it, I felt compelled to tell you, and now I've done that. Are you ready for the third thing?"

"Sure."

"I've just been talking about Paris with your son's steady, and something occurred to me, which I wanted to share with you."

"All right."

"When I came to Paris for the first time, do you remember what I told you about it? About how it felt to be here?"

"I remember you telling me."

"Oh, you remember something? How nice that is for you. And me. It's nice for both of us. Hail, hail."

Franklin cleared his throat but didn't speak.

"Well," Frances said. "I've figured out what I was startled by."

"What's that?"

"I recognized Paris as the eventual location of my death."

Franklin paused. "And what does that mean?"

"Just what I said. Something in the sight of this city sent up

an alert. Now I understand what startled me was a presenti-
ment of what was to come, do you see? Of what's coming now."

"You're planning on dying soon, is that what you're telling me?"

Frances said, "We're both going to be dead quite soon,
Frank, yes."

The sentence hung there. "Frances," Franklin said. She
reached over and blinked the light shut between her forefinger
and thumb.

She thanked Madeleine for her assistance and instructed
her to go back to sleep. Madeleine returned to her foam pad
but Frances remained in the bathroom. She began running a
bath, while Madeleine lay on the pad, staring at the ceiling and
wondering what she should do. She knew by the fact of her
greenness that Frances could not be helped, and yet, she felt an
obligation to act in some way. Her head was pounding, and an
ill-defined nausea lingered at the edge of her every breath. She
stood and returned to the bathroom, knocking softly. The door
opened a crack.

"I'm going to wake up Malcolm," she said.

"Then I'll lock the door. I only need a moment, you know."

Madeleine said, "You can't expect me to sit by like this."

Frances thought about it, and it seemed she agreed with
what Madeleine was saying. "Why don't you leave?" she said.
"I'll wait until after you go, all right?"

Frances shut the door and Madeleine went back to her pad.
She was thinking of something that had happened years before
in a park in downtown Los Angeles.

She'd been sitting on a bench eating her lunch when a young
man walked past and sat on the bench beside hers. He looked

troubled, and she spied on him, looking sideways at his stern profile. There came into his face the green coloring; it would rise and retreat, vanish, then reappear. He sat suddenly upright and the greenness flared, bright and constant, now. He stood and walked from the park and Madeleine watched as he crossed Wilshire, disappearing into the mouth of a beige stucco apartment building. A long moment passed before Madeleine heard the muffled clap of a gunshot from deep within the building. A woman shrieked; Madeleine went away.

Frances turned off the bath. Madeleine packed her bag and left the apartment.

# 41.

Stepping onto the sidewalk she saw the mangy figure of Small Frank sitting at the edge of the park across the street and looking up at the apartment. Madeleine crossed over to meet him, but upon noticing her approach he trotted away, out of reach. She paused, then came nearer a second time; again Small Frank retreated, disappearing fully into the darkness of the park, now. Madeleine was considering following after him when she understood all at once how absurd the scenario had become. She decided she'd had more than enough of this group, and she turned and walked away in the direction of a taxi stand up the road. After she'd gone, Small Frank returned to his initial position in the park and resumed his study of the apartment.

# 42.

Frances eased into the bath without removing her dress. A box cutter lay on the lip of the bathtub and she watched it awhile. She took it up and drew a line with the blade from the left wrist to the crook of her arm. She drew the same line on her right wrist, then submerged both arms in the warm water. There was pain at the start, a very awful, stinging pain, but then there came a numbness, and after that a knowledge of calm, which in turn grew to something like rapture. It was in the room with her; it was behind her; it was at her shoulder. Her heart was sprinting and blood issued from her wrists in pulsations, an image that put Frances in mind of beta fish streaming from her body. An exclamatory brightness saturated the field of her mind and in the moment preceding death she felt heroic. She suspected this a trick of the heart, one final deception before the void announced itself, but she went along with it, wanting to be game. Was there anything worse in the world than a poor sport?

But are not
all Facts Dreams
as soon as
we put
them behind
us—

—*Emily Dickinson*

# CODA

Mme Reynard was making coffee for the policemen. She had been the one to find Frances early that morning. Her reaction was surprising: she was perfectly composed and single-minded about it. She telephoned the authorities and waited silently with Frances. She looked at the corpse from time to time but said nothing to it and understood it was no longer her friend. When the police arrived, she brought them to the body, then moved alone to Malcolm's bedroom, waking him and Susan. "Your mother has killed herself in the night," she said. "The police are here to take care of her. You are going to be all right, Malcolm. You just are."

"Where," asked Malcolm, standing.

"She's in the bath but I wish you wouldn't go and I'm asking you please not to."

He did go, and the sight of his mother sitting upright in the still, red water folded his legs for him, and he sat down roughly on the tile floor. A policeman assisted him in standing and led him to the sofa in the living room. A cup of coffee was placed in his hand but he didn't drink it. Susan sat beside him, saying nothing, holding his arm. Joan was crying in the bedroom; Julius and Mme Reynard were in the kitchen giving statements to the lead detective, a calm, attentive man named Alphonse. Three policemen stood in a group by the living room window, talking in low tones about something other than what had occurred, was occurring in the apartment.

Detective Alphonse asked Malcolm to come to the station headquarters with him. Malcolm agreed and they left together, walking without speaking. Malcolm was wearing the houndstooth trench coat Frances had bought him when they'd arrived.

Detective Alphonse's office was not the dingy chamber of television drama but a tidy, airy space with skylights and a number of thriving plants hanging from the ceiling. He asked Malcolm if he wanted a coffee and Malcolm said he did and Detective Alphonse called for two, which were delivered by a uniformed policeman who did not address Malcolm or even look at him. After he left, the detective and Malcolm sat in further silence, taking sips of their coffee at intervals.

Detective Alphonse began speaking about his history, his youth. As an adolescent, he said, he'd been a fan of crime. He followed criminal news as his friends did the football scores. "I came to learn this is common in my profession," he said. "The interest is simply there in certain of us, and from an early age. A very specific social deformity." The detective had known a glint of recognition when he came on shift that morning and heard the name Frances Price. He looked into it and realized he had followed the case of Franklin Price in his early twenties. It had been a sort of sensation in France, possessing all the noirish American elements a crime-hungry heart could hope for—the deceased millionaire, the chic widow, and at the center loomed the great mystery of: Why had she left him like that? And to go skiing, no less? Had she gone mad? Or had he deserved such an end?

Detective Alphonse didn't ask Malcolm any of these questions, naturally; he only referenced a familiarity with Malcolm's family history. Malcolm seemed hardly to hear him. He sat staring at his feet; realizing his shoes were untied, he tied them. When he finished this, Detective Alphonse told him, "Mr. Price, a mystery has occurred in Paris, France. I am paid a wage that I should illuminate the mystery so much as I can. Of course, you're under no obligation to answer any of my questions. But it would be helpful to me if you would."

Malcolm said, "You can ask me whatever you want."

Detective Alphonse took up a pen and flipped open his notebook. "What is your age?"

"Thirty-two."

"And your mother's age?"

"Sixty-five."

"What is your place of residence?"

"We've been living at Joan's apartment, here in Paris. Before that we were in Manhattan."

Detective Alphonse asked for their respective US addresses and Malcolm named the Upper East Side address. "You and your mother lived together?"

"Yes."

"Was she unwell?"

"No. We lived together because we wanted to."

"Had you lived apart in the past?"

"They kept me at boarding school until my father died. Since then I've been with her."

Detective Alphonse asked, "Did you anticipate this from your mother?"

"I'm unsurprised that she's done it. But I wasn't prepared for the sight."

"Had she been despondent recently?"

"I don't know if I'd use the word despondent. She's been acting weird since the money ran out."

"Did your money run out?"

"It did."

Detective Alphonse wrote out a long sentence, nodding to himself. "And she's been emotional?"

"Not in the way you mean. Actually she's been abnormally friendly. She always avoided strangers and hangers-on, but in the last weeks she became sort of a joiner."

"Interesting," Detective Alphonse said.

"Is it?"

"Is it not?" The detective took a breath. "Something delicate."

"What's that?"

"Did your mother ever discuss the details of the death of your father?"

"Here and there she did."

"Do you have any idea why she behaved that way?"

"Which way?"

"Why she didn't, for example, call the authorities?"

Malcolm said, "What I know is that she felt strongly apart from him, then."

"Strongly apart." Detective Alphonse wrote down these

words and underlined them. He said, "I'd think that would be a burdensome thing to carry about for the rest of one's life? Her having done that, I mean."

"I don't know if it was."

"No?"

"Anyway I never noticed it as a burden."

"So you don't believe there's a connection between your father's death and your mother's suicide?"

"No."

"Why did she do it, do you think?"

Malcolm thought for a while. "Aesthetic preference," he said finally. He frowned. "What will they do with her body? I'd like her removed from the bath as quickly as possible."

"I imagine they've already removed her, Mr. Price. They'll take her to the morgue. It's not far from here. You can see her whenever you wish."

"I don't want to see her, I just want them to take her out of the bath."

"They'll clean her and dress her injuries."

Malcolm shook his head. "Fine," he said.

Detective Alphonse studied his notes. He had no other questions, and really, there were none that had needed answering in the first place. In the case of a suicide, the collection of data surrounding the event was often interesting but not requisite, from a legal standpoint. He put the cap on his pen and looked up. Malcolm was opening his mouth to speak: "My mother was overfine for this world, Detective Alphonse. That's what damaged her. She belonged to another time and it was her ugly luck to be born among us."

Detective Alphonse shut his notebook and stood. "Thank

you for speaking with me," he said. "You have my card, and I
hope you'll tell me if there's anything I can help you with. Please
let me know if you decide to leave Paris."

"Thank you, I will. Goodbye."

"Goodbye."

Malcolm left the police station and walked toward Joan's
apartment. The sidewalks were overrun with people hurrying to
work; Malcolm stepped off the curb and walked in the street to
avoid them. He had always, since the first time he visited Paris,
felt he was invisible there. It was a feeling he loved very much.

He was aware of being in an intermediate period: he hadn't
yet recognized Frances's death but sensed the recognition's even
approach. He sat on a bench across from the square at Saint-
Sulpice. He couldn't latch on to any particular thought or emotion for a while; then he began thinking of the morning Frances
came for him at the academy.

Malcolm was summoned from his classroom and arrived
at the headmaster's office to find her bantering with the man
about the protocol of removing Malcolm from school. She had
a sheaf of papers in front of her, which she regarded with dis-
taste. Looking up, she greeted Malcolm and explained her wish
to take him away. Her eyes were glassy and she smelled of cigarettes.

"Is there anything you want from your room?" she asked.

"Clothes," he said.

"I'll buy you new clothes. Is there anything else?"

"No."

"Good. Let's go."

"But the forms, Mrs. Price," said the headmaster.

"Why don't you be a champion and fill them out for me?"

"No, it's not for me to do."

"Well, I don't want to, and I'm not going to, and I'm afraid that concludes the tune. Good morning."

Malcolm stood gawking at the headmaster. How novel it was to see this fearsome man on the defensive. Frances gave Malcolm a friendly shove and they exited the office, walking down the hall and toward the entrance. They crossed the court-yard to the waiting Rolls.

"Where's the driver?" asked Malcolm.

"Driver quit." Frances stopped to light a cigarette: *click!* "I'm the driver."

"I thought you didn't know how to drive."

"It's pretty self-explanatory. Sit up front and keep me company."

She drove down the gravel road. Pebbles were pinging off the Rolls's undercarriage and the leaden car fishtailed around corners. They came to a paved two-lane highway; Frances accelerated and the sedan crouched nearer the ground.

She asked Malcolm, "So, how was it?"

"How was what?"

She jerked her thumb back. "Your educational experience."

"I don't know," he said.

"Don't say 'I don't know.' Of course you know. What was it like?"

"Not really very much fun," said Malcolm.

"Didn't you have any friends?"

"Some."

"But you found the relationships unfulfilling?"

Malcolm was going to say he didn't know but caught himself. He looked at his mother and shrugged.

"What was the food like?" she asked.

"The food was awful."

She held her palm out flat. "Give me your tie."

"Why?"

She continued holding out her hand. Malcolm undid his tie and gave it to her and she threw it out the window. Malcolm turned to watch it whipping in the wake of the Rolls. Soon they entered into a dense forest. There were no other cars on the darkened road. "Your father's dead," Frances said.

"I know."

"How do you know?"

"The other kids showed it to me in the paper."

"What did it say about him?"

"That he died a few days ago."

"That's true. What else did it say?"

Malcolm folded his hands together and rested them on his lap.

"What did it say about me?" she asked.

The question made Malcolm shy.

"It's okay, go ahead," Frances said.

Malcolm said, "You were arrested, it said. Because you didn't do what you were supposed to do."

Frances muttered to herself, lighting a cigarette off another and tossing the short butt out the window. "Look," she said. "They didn't know your father, and they certainly don't know me, and it's boorish, typically boorish of them to state the terms of what should have been done in an episode they could never guess at. What was and was not done was done or not done for a very good, a very real reason, all right?"

"All right."

"What you need to understand is that I wasn't wrong," she said. "If this is going to work—you and me, I mean—you're going to have to take my word for that. Okay?"

Malcolm nodded. "Okay," he said. In a little while he asked, "What was jail like?"

Frances was tapping the steering wheel. "Not really very much fun."

"How was the food?"

Frances nodded approvingly. "You're getting it."

They exited the forest and emerged into sunshine. To the side of them lay undulating fields of grass. Frances flicked the cigarette out the window and rolled it up tight, smoke floating in the Rolls. "Are you going to have to go back to jail?" Malcolm asked.

Frances considered the question. "I don't think so," she said. The road banked south and they followed the line, moving toward Manhattan.

Malcolm was pulled from this reverie by the faint scent of flowers. The smell was similar to a perfume Frances had worn; he suddenly had the feeling she was there with him now—that she was visiting him. The scent of flowers became stronger, and now Malcolm sensed she was standing behind him. He was frightened by the thought; he turned slowly around to face her. But Frances was not there. Malcolm found himself looking at a florist's storefront. For no good reason, and just to do something, he stood and entered.

The shop was dim, the air dense with moisture. The displays were soothing in a small and wanted way. When the clerk moved to stand beside Malcolm, he pointed. "I'll take those ones."

"How many?"

"A big armful."

Malcolm made his purchase and exited the florist's. He was a young man without socks on walking in the golden, late-morning Parisian sun with a bouquet of pink ranunculus in his arms. He looked down at them, admiring them, and wondering who they were for. They were for Susan, he decided. He imagined her face when he passed them over. She would be confused by the gesture, but later, in remembering the moment, wouldn't she be pleased? Malcolm wanted to be kind to Susan.

He felt nimble as he navigated the sidewalk, moving around the bodies, men and women alone in their minds, freighted with their intimate informations. Crossing the square at Saint-Sulpice, he split through a stream of nuns, who, as insects interrupted, lost the scent of their paths and spun away in eddies.

# ACKNOWLEDGMENTS

Phil, Emma, Nina, and Leonard Aronson, David Berman, Suet Yee Chong, Caspian Dennis, Gary deWitt, Gustavo deWitt, Mike deWitt, Nick deWitt, Susan deWitt, Emma Dries, Ashley Garland, Sammy Harkham, Alexa von Hirschberg, Alexandra Pringle, Andy Hunter, Eric Isaacson, Azazel Jacobs, Megan Lynch, Sarah MacLachlan, Peter McGuigan and all at Foundry, Laura Meyer, Brian Mumford, Leslie Napoles, Rene Navarrette, Max Porter, Jon Raymond, Kelly Reichardt, Shelley Short, all at the Sou'Wester, Antoine Tanguay, Marie-Catherine Vacher, Libby Werbel, Janie Yoon. Special thanks to Emahoy Tsegue-Mariam Guebru.

© Kelly Reichardt

PATRICK DeWITT was born on Vancouver Island in 1975. He is the author of the critically acclaimed novels *Undermajordomo Minor*, *Ablutions*, and *The Sisters Brothers*, which won the Governor General's Literary Award for Fiction, the Rogers Writers' Trust Fiction Prize, and the Stephen Leacock Medal, and was a finalist for the Man Booker Prize and the Scotiabank Giller Prize. *The Sisters Brothers* has also been adapted into a major motion picture directed by Palme d'Or winner Jacques Audiard. DeWitt lives in Portland, Oregon.